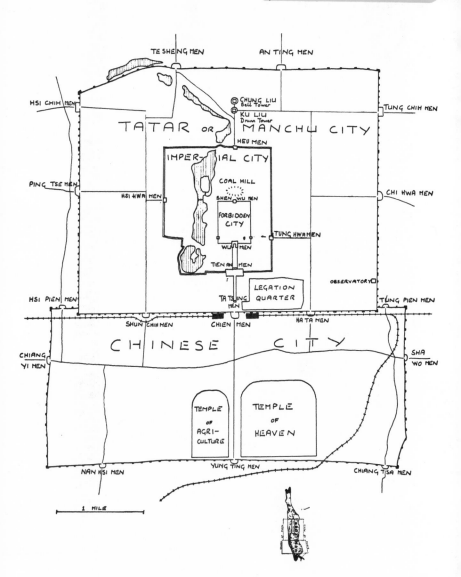

TE SHENG MEN

AN TING MEN

HSI CHIH MEN

TUNG CHIH MEN

◎ CHUNG LIU
Bell Tower

KU LIU
Drum Tower

TATAR OR MANCHU CITY

HEU MEN

IMPER-IAL CITY

PING TSE MEN

COAL HILL

HSI HWA MEN

SHEN WU MEN

CHI HWA MEN

FORBIDDEN CITY

TUNG HWA MEN

WU MEN

TIEN AN MEN

OBSERVATORY ☐

HSI PIEN MEN

TA TSING MEN

LEGATION QUARTER

TUNG PIEN MEN

SHUN CHIH MEN

CHIEN MEN

HA TA MEN

CHINESE CITY

CHIANG YI MEN

SHA WO MEN

TEMPLE OF AGRI-CULTURE

TEMPLE OF HEAVEN

NAN HSI MEN

YUNG TING MEN

CHIANG TSA MEN

1 MILE

RENÉ LEYS

RENÉ LEYS

A Novel by Victor Segalen

Translated from the French by J.A. Underwood

The Overlook Press
Woodstock, New York

First published in 1988 by
The Overlook Press
Lewis Hollow Road
Woodstock, New York 12498

Library of Congress Cataloging-in-Publication Data

Segalen, Victor, 1878–1919.
  René Leys.

  I. Title.
PQ2637.E33R413   1988   843'.912   88-42723
ISBN: 0-87951-324-1 (cloth)
ISBN: 0-87951-350-0 (paper)

Introduction

Victor Segalen was born at Brest in Brittany on 14 January 1878. There was something of a naval tradition in the family, particularly on his mother's side, and in 1898 he applied to and was accepted for the Naval Medical College in Bordeaux. His four years in Bordeaux saw a widening of his interests in music and literature. He became an ardent admirer of Debussy, whose music was then enjoying its first popularity (the two men were later to collaborate on a project for an opera, which the outbreak of the First World War prevented them from completing); in literature it was Huysmans who first fired his imagination, and through a mutual friend he was able to meet the author of *Against Nature* and *The Cathedral,* a meeting that gave further impetus to Segalen's growing interest in mysticism, the exotic, and pathological mental phenomena. His thesis dealt with the medical description of such phenomena in the literature of the Naturalist school and as such is almost a symbol of the double nature of Segalen's career from this point on.

In 1902 he qualified as a naval doctor and was posted to the *Durance,* then stationed at Tahiti. He traveled *via* New York and San Francisco, where he was held up for some months by an almost fatal attack of typhoid fever. It was while convalescing from this illness that Segalen made his first contact—in the

microcosmic form of San Francisco's "Chinatown"—with the
country that was to play such a decisive part in his life.

Segalen spent one and a half years in Polynesia. Based on
Tahiti, the *Durance* made patrols as far afield as New Caledonia
in one direction and the Marquesas in the other, reaching the
latter only three months after Gauguin's death. Segalen visited
the hut where Gauguin had spent the last months of his life, met
the artist's servant Tioka, who told him, referring to Gauguin,
that "there is no more man now," and attended the auction of
Gauguin's effects, where he purchased (for a mere seven francs)
the artist's last great painting, *Breton Village in the Snow* (now
in the Louvre, Paris), which the auctioneer had presented to a
hilarious audience upside-down as "Niagara Falls." The life and
work of the great artist-recluse made a deep impression on the
young ship's doctor and provided one of the sources of inspira-
tion for *Les Immémoriaux* (1907), Segalen's first major literary
work and the fruit of his experiences among the Polynesian
islanders.

In 1904 the *Durance* was ordered back to France, sailing
by way of the East Indies, Ceylon, and the Red Sea. At Djibouti
Segalen came upon the traces of another great artist who had
spent the latter part of his life in self-imposed exile—though
not, as in Gauguin's case, in order to find his art, but in order to
forget it. Rimbaud's influence on modern poetry has been of the
same order as Gauguin's upon modern art, yet when he died in
1891 at the age of thirty-seven he had written nothing for the
last fifteen years. At Djibouti they remembered him only as an
explorer, trader, and occasional trafficker in arms. The paradox
of Rimbaud's existence gave the nascent writer further food for
thought.

Back in France in 1905, Segalen married and settled down
in a shore posting at Brest, spending all his free time working
on the notes and projects he had brought back from his trip
round the world, his efforts culminating in 1907 in the publica-
tion of *Les Immémoriaux,* a historical "novel" (really the book
does not fit into any rigid category; Segalen submitted it for the

Prix Goncourt, for which under the terms of Edmond de Goncourt's will only novels are eligible, but he never in fact called it a novel himself, as he did *René Leys,* for example) about the people of Tahiti in the early part of the nineteenth century. Among the many new friends he made during this period was the poet and novelist Gilbert de Voisins, with whom he began to plan his next venture into the world of the exotic—an expedition into the interior of China. He started studying Chinese intensively and in less than a year was able to pass the Navy's examination as a "cadet interpreter," thus qualifying for a two-year posting in China during which his only duty was "to perfect his knowledge and command of the language." On 12 June 1909 he arrived in Peking (or "Pei-king," as Segalen more correctly transcribes it in *René Leys*), "Northern Capital" of the country in which he was to spend half of the ten years remaining to him and which was to reveal to him his poetic vocation and inspire his finest works.

Peking in 1909, nine years after the Boxer Rising, was a city in which Europeans enjoyed a charmed existence. Dowager Empress Tzu Hsi (1835–1908), who had fanned the xenophobic flame behind the "Society of Harmonious Fists" and thus indirectly provoked the humiliating sack of the capital by a six-nation force in 1900, had died the year before. So had her nephew and prisoner, the young Emperor Kuang Hsu (1874–1908), whose attempts to introduce a measure of reform into the corrupt Manchu administration in 1898 she had so effectively throttled. The new emperor, P'u-i, having been less than two years old at the time of his accession, his father, Prince Chun, ruled the empire in his name. One of the Regent's first acts had been to avenge his brother, the late emperor, by depriving of office the man who had betrayed him in 1898 and connived at Tzu Hsi's keeping him a prisoner for the rest of his days. The man was Yuan Shih-kai, the Ch'ing dynasty's last "strong man," whose own vengeance was to take the form of bringing that dynasty's almost three centuries of rule to an end in 1912. When Segalen came to Peking, however, the revolution lay two years in the future. The Manchu conquerors were still enthroned behind the purple walls of the Forbidden City, ruling their Chinese subjects with a rod not of iron so much as of silver, more or less the entire administration of the empire being founded on peculation.

Returning to Peking early in 1910 from the expedition into the interior with Gilbert de Voisins, Segalen settled with his wife and small son, who had meanwhile come out to join him, in the house in the Tatar City described in *René Leys*. It was soon after this that he made the acquaintance of a young Frenchman by the name of Maurice Roy. At nineteen Roy spoke perfect Pekingese and Segalen enthusiastically employed him as tutor and mentor of his efforts to plumb the secrets of this land that had taken such a hold on his imagination. In almost everything except the final dramatic turn that Segalen gives his novel, Maurice Roy *is* René Leys. Segalen kept a diary of the young man's progressively more astonishing revelations about the inmates of the Forbidden City, last scions of a doomed dynasty, and of his own intimate relations with them.[1] When he came to write the novel two years later (after the revolution and the abdication), everything except the polish, as it were, was already present in his *Secret Annals according to M.R.* But it is precisely this polish that makes *René Leys* one of the most original novels of its period and gives it even today, *three-quarters of a century* after it was written, such a modern feeling.

Victor Segalen had very decided views about the craft of fiction as practiced by his contemporaries. In fact, he wrote *René Leys* as a result of a bet—a bet that he could write a successful novel that was entirely without "plot." What he despised above all in the novels of his day was "the author . . . that hateful character . . . who so improbably knows so many things, and lays them immodestly before us; of whose presence one is constantly aware, often without his once having the guts to appear."[1a] *René Leys* begins as the story of "the book that never was," a confession of the author's failure to achieve his purpose of gaining entry to the Imperial Palace, the "Within." It continues as a kind of thriller that its author is constantly disowning. It ends, with a breathtaking shock of logic, in a nostalgic acceptance of fiction as situated—comfortably or disturbingly—midway between reality and the imagination, and of the longed-for "Within" as lying eternally out of reach. Though Segalen's reputation rests primarily on his poetry—*Stèles* (1912), *Peintures* (1916), *Odes* (published posthumously in 1926), *Equipée* (1920)—he left in *René Leys* a novel that is both an original contribution to the genre and a moving, engrossing, and thought-provoking work in its own right. "A parody of the detective story, a diary of a stay in Peking, a meditation on the Imagination, *René Leys* is also, and primarily, like Kafka's *The Castle*, an allegorical novel of Being, the eternally absent. Beneath a mask of irony Segalen poured into this book all the anguish of man in thrall to his limitations and tortured by his insatiable hunger after secrets. This is the novel of the Impossibility of Knowing" (Henry Bouillier).

Shortly after completing *René Leys* Segalen left Peking on a further archaeological expedition into the interior, which was brought to a premature end by the outbreak of the war. He was recalled to France and at his own request posted to the front near Dunkerque. His health was already beginning to deteriorate at this time, and after some months in the hospital he returned to an administrative job in Brest. Towards the end of 1916, however, impatient once more for the physical action that he regarded his whole life long as the indispensable prelude to all spiritual or artistic effort, he accepted a post as doctor to a labor-recruiting mission about to leave for China. The mission was something of a failure but Segalen took advantage of this last stay in China to pursue his researches in archaeology—a field in which he made an important contribution to Sinological studies.

On his way back to France at the beginning of 1918 Segalen was in excellent spirits. "Last night I celebrated my fortieth birthday," he wrote to his wife, "an occasion that finds me in first-class shape. Not a single gray hair—discounting the twenty-fifth up from the ankle on my right calf . . . I have three plays, ten novels, four essays, two theories of the world, one tome each on poetics, exoticism, and aesthetics, a treatise on the Beyond, a comprehensive catalogue of things unknown, twenty or so other works that defy classification, and four thousand and sixty-three articles of between two hundred and two thousand lines apiece to write before I can really retire . . ." Yet little more than a year later he was writing to a friend, "My body has become a craven traitor to me. It has been causing me concern for some time, but at least it always obeyed me; I have dragged it through a fair number of adventures for which it did not appear to be cut out. But for the last five or six years I have been doing so at the expense of an energy that, although spontaneous, was also conscious; a case of wear without repair . . . I am suffering from no known illness . . . yet it is exactly as if I were seriously ill. I have given up weighing myself. I am taking no more medicines. I simply note the fact that life is slipping away from me."

Exactly a month later, on 21 May 1919, while out walking in the Forest of Huelgoat where he had played as a boy, Victor Segalen died. He had not accomplished all that his phenomenal will set out to accomplish, but he had made lasting contributions to literature and archaeology and had added a significant chapter to the ongoing story of the meeting of East and West.

J.A. Underwood

To his memory
V. S.

RENE LEYS

I shall know no more, then. Well, I shall not insist; I shall retire from the field . . . respectfully, let it be said, and of course backwards, since court etiquette will have it so, and since it is a question of the Imperial Palace, and of an audience that was never granted, and that never will be granted . . .

It is with this admission—ridiculous or diplomatic, depending on the tone you attribute to it—that I must close, having only just opened it, this journal of which I had hoped to make a book. The book, too, will never be. (But failing the book, what a splendid posthumous title—*The Book That Never Was!*)

I thought I had it "in the bag"—more "consummate," more saleable than any novel ever copyrighted, more "substantial" than any other collection of so-called human documents. Better than any imaginary account it would have gripped its readers, at each of its leaps into reality, with all of the magic contained within those walls . . . where I shall never enter.

No one can deny that, in terms of mystery, Pei-king is a superb "production." To begin with, the triple plan of its cities obeys neither the dictates of the cadastral assembly nor the lodging requirements of such as feed and breed. The capital of the greatest empire under the sun was conceived for its own sake, laid out like a chessboard in the far north of the Yellow Plain, girt with geometrical walls, ruled with avenues, cross-ruled with alleys running at right-angles, and raised in one monumental sweep . . . and then, afterwards, occupied, eventually to overflowing in the seedier quarters, by its parasites, the Chinese people. The principal square, however, the Tatar/Manchu City, still harbors the conquerors—and this dream . . .

Inside, deep in the innermost center of the Palace, a face: a child-man, and Emperor, Lord of the Sun and Son of Heaven (whom everyone, including journalists, insists on referring to as "Kuang Hsu," which actually designates the period of his reign, that is to say A.D. 1874–1908). His real name, his name during his lifetime, was the unutterable . . . *Himself*—and it not being permitted me to give the *name,* I give the European *pronoun* all the reverential emphasis of the Manchu gesture (the two sleeves raised with joined fists to meet the lowered forehead) which designates him—Himself remains the figure and incarnate symbol of the most pathetic and most mortal of creatures. Impossible deeds are ascribed to him . . . and perhaps he really and truly performed them. I am convinced he died as none die nowadays—of ten entirely natural ailments but primarily of that eleventh (unrecognized) ailment of being Emperor—that is to say the victim appointed for the last four thousand years as intercessory sacrifice between Heaven and the People on earth.

. . . And the place of his sacrifice, the precinct within which his person was immured, the Purple and Forbidden City —which now raises its ramparts against me—became the only possible stage for this drama, this story, this book which, without Himself, has no further justification . . .

And yet I have made every effort to muster his Presence, to round up without the walls all the retrospective glimpses of the "Within." In this I relied upon the professional acumen of our European doctors. For there they sit, lining the "Street of the Legations," hard by the outfall of the Palace sewers, ready to creep through every crack and, once inside, to sink their fraternal teeth into any colleague who seeks to follow. One day it is the doctor of such and such a country whose services are called upon, and from then on that country's Legation will boast of being in charge—sole charge—of Their Imperial Healths. Two or even more of these learned "D. Pills" will flatter themselves simultaneously that they alone have been summoned and consulted, to the comprehensive disparagement of all the rest, and they will look at one another with unsmiling faces. It was through them I had to make my approach. I feared I might be offending against medical secrecy, but they furnished me with nothing but a few professional indiscretions . . . Their reports were scrawled on the same paper and couched in the same long-winded, prophylactic language they use to bamboozle and condemn their bourgeois clients. They imputed to Himself, The Unique One, the kind of infantile taints that any common brat may throw in his parents' face . . . They diagnosed de-gen-er-a-ti-on . . . The Son of Heaven, in a word, was suffering from a *hereditary* disease!

Repelled by the sacrilegious ignorance of my compatriots, I turned to the native Eunuchs. They are a different kind of brotherhood—as honorable, but more exclusive. It is by no means open to all; you must have your diploma. Its offices are all restrictive—with certain amendments. Paternity, for example, is permitted at the higher levels, and perfidy at all levels.

I tried bribing one of these characters. The return was not worth the outlay: a number of well-worn anecdotes that had already spiced the columns of the local press before I received them—nothing, in other words, that could really be described as a "secret of the bed-chamber." Not that I blame my Eunuchs: the "bed-chamber," as classically defined by curtains and *ruelle,* very likely does not exist in the Palace.

There remained the Chinese physicians. Armed with foreign prescriptions yet faithful to the autochthonous pharmacopoeia, they are extremely proud of the two-edged sword of their formidable science. One of the best of them, after a good dinner

—it too an equal mixture of French and Pekingese *cuisine*—at my house, was pleased to relate, act out, and bring to life before my eyes this scene: a consultation in the heart of the Palace.

The consultant is kneeling on the floor with head bowed, having completed his thrice three prostrations. The Emperor, and the fearsome old Dowager, are seated above the level of all eyes. The consultant, on being questioned, dare not open his mouth to speak. He is coerced. Most respectfully he inquires "in which portion of the Precious Body the Ineffable Person is unjustly indisposed . . ."

The August Crone replies on behalf of Himself that "the humors are fretting beneath the skin . . ."

The consultant respectfully recommends some medicaments, he has forgotten what (certainly not a foreign drug!—he would have been accused of treason, of intent to poison; even less a Chinese powder!—having been summoned for his foreign know-how).

He recalled very precisely, however, the following subjective impression:

"His head did not appear to me to rest over-solidly on his shoulders . . ."

That he remembered. I congratulated him. But that was all.

That has been all. Should I throw in my hand? I am giving myself one last chance to penetrate the Within—using the medium of its language, the difficult "Northern Mandarin." From now on I shall employ no intermediaries, no eunuchs; I shall wait for the opportunity that shall enable me first-hand to . . . say, or do . . . what? I have no idea.

At all events I am clinging to this chance and have thrown myself with the energy of despair into the vocabulary of the "Kuan Hua." It is commonly said that one must dedicate one's whole life to it, from childhood to old age, to be able to write and compose like a graduate from the provinces, and this may be so. Actually I find it comes out quite easily. I am conscious of my prowess. I can chat away, I can hold a conversation, I can already say almost *anything*. I do not know whom I should congratulate—myself, the language, or my tutor. Against all the dictates of logic I have chosen for my tutor, here in the middle of China, a foreigner, an illiterate barbarian, and what is worse, a young Belgian![2] I was much struck by his extraordinary talent for picking up anything and everything, and perhaps for passing it on. Officially he holds a chair of "Political Economy" at the College of Nobles. Anywhere else this would worry me . . . But we have agreed that, in the interests of mutual comprehension, we will speak only Chinese.

My tutor would be extremely surprised to learn the true objective of my sessions with him. He is the dutiful son of an excellent grocer of the Legation Quarter. I failed to recognize him beside the paternal scales. Yet he speaks with such respect of his father, business, the family, "savings," servants, carriages, horses, and his father's principles that he clearly believes it impossible to lead, in Pei-king, a more honorable life than his father leads . . . As regards literature, he is rereading Paul Féval.[3]

If I succeed, if I reach . . . there where I despair of reaching—he shall be the first I shall surprise with my success—and alarm by revealing his share in it . . . although, as I have said already, it is unlikely that I shall succeed.

He is a good tutor. I have engaged him for another month of lessons. And I hereby declare in advance that I renounce all expectations.

So be it. I now no longer have *one* tutor in Pekingese but two. It happened in spite of myself and is, I believe, a matter for congratulation. The good man made a deep impression on me. I have begun to have hopes again. Supposing I were to find through his good offices my very own way into the Within! Oh, by the straightest gate, admittedly, the tradesman's entrance, almost next-door to the kitchens . . . This gate is now open to me against (for everything has its price here) the modest sum of ten silver taels per month and an hour and a half's (worthwhile or wasted) time per day.

    This genuine "scholar" presented himself in the guise of a little, ageless man with short legs—and with his face, which was the very image of politeness, bowed towards the floor. I remember noticing his amazing umbrella—also ageless, and purposeless. He offered me—for all the world like some Colombo dealer in moonstones and false topaz—a sheaf of soiled French visiting-cards. Numbers of my compatriots had made the experiment and found his scholarship extensive, his method lucid, and his patience protracted . . . in fine, he felt a loyal affection for the French and had done so since the time when, compromised in the Boxer affair, and drawn abruptly towards Catholicism, he had for that very reason come to us for asylum.

Would he, I wondered, be asking asylum of me again? Everything is so quiet in Pei-king at the moment!

He knows nothing of my language. I brought out without a blush such words of his as I could recollect, and I gathered, thanks to the intervention of my boy, that he has been teaching Northern Mandarin or "Kuan Hua" for many years at a police college attached to the Palace—and that he owed his appointment to relatives of his wife, a Manchu and "Lady-in-Waiting of the Eighth Class" to the Seventh Concubine during the Hsien Feng period[4] . . . (Second Empire! That makes her no chicken!) He himself is a "Chinese of the Banners," a descendant of those valiant sons of Han who rallied early to the Manchu cause, judging it opportune to give their first allegiance to the Conquerors. There were further confidences, though I cannot swear to having translated them accurately . . . But of this much I am certain: he teaches or has taught in the internal police force of the Palace . . . He even added a word which might have been "secret."

This is really getting in by the back door! But get in I will, and I believe I have done well to engage him right away to give me the benefit of his advice. In order to spare the susceptibilities which I imagine he has in common with his compatriots regarding the good faith of my people, I have decided to take precautions against his meeting my first tutor, the little Belgian, here in my house. One reads so much about the exquisite wariness of these Chinese . . .

Will my next step be to dismiss the little Belgian?

No. It will do if I can account for his presence here with the aid of a few lies and polite formulae. He can have some unobjectionable job . . . he can be my secretary . . . or, more conveniently, my friend. Yes, that will be fine. I have no idea how you say "secretary" in Chinese, whereas it has long been my habit to fling about rather at random the benedictory epithet "friend."

But it will be best to make sure they never meet. For one thing they would start jabbering away under my very nose with a facility which would turn me green with envy, using turns of phrase far above a beginner's head, communicating in a veritable verbal shorthand which I should find positively infuriating. And for another my Belgian might begin to question my Chinese of the Banners about his job—about his professional functions in a college attached to the Palace—a police college . . . Yes, now I am sure I heard him say "secret police." And here discretion is clearly *de rigueur*.

No, clearly they must never bump into one another here.

Here, on the other hand, is a newcomer whom I need have no qualms in introducing to my future Manchu connections. For a start he introduced himself to me, quite unsolicited, through the agency of a double-sided visiting-card. On the Chinese side I was proud to be able to decipher one of the characters of his name, the most considerable of his titles—"clerk at the Ministry of Communications"—and, without complicated hesitation, his address, differing as it does in no more than a cardinal point from my own. In fact we live in the same street, the same *hutung*, his address being "North Gate" and mine the southern alignment. We are neighbors, and it is to this fortuitous circumstance that I owed his visit. But all I could think of at the time and can think of now is: this man is "something" at the Ministry of Communications!

I was anxious that he should take a seat. He had already done so. Settling himself down with a snort, he began to hold forth. He was delighted, he told me, to have "unearthed" a Frenchman who appeared to take an interest in the Chinese ... He repeated this sentiment.

"Sir, they're damned rare birds in these parts!"

"I'm sorry—Frenchmen?"

"No! People who take an interest in the Chinese. When I

saw you descend on us in this out-of-the-way quarter and take a house near the Observatory, I could tell right off you understood China."

"So soon?"

"Mind you, I've been here almost ten years and three months myself."

"And three months ... You count the months?"

"Had to," he declared complacently. "No alternative. Absolutely essential for my affairs."

I had no wish to hear details.

He went on, "I maintain, d'you see, that the only way to deal with the Chinese is in the Chinese fashion. Otherwise you're wasting your time ... They don't trust you ... You'll never get anything out of them ..."

Don't I know it!

"I've gone about things differently. To start with, I came to live in the Tatar City as you've done yourself. I have my servants and I pay them the Chinese rate—three dollars. I have mules—no horses!—my Chinese cart ..."

He added familiarly, "I have my women."

This failed to dazzle me. I have sampled the kind of female companionship that Pei-king, the "Northern Capital," places at the disposal of its distinguished guests and people who are passing through ... Just north of the Legation Quarter ... No doubt this gentleman was offering ...

"I've just married one."

"You've ..."

I looked up. The newlywed's face was a picture of contented propriety. My deepest apologies for having thought he was procuring ...

I concluded, "Are you only marrying one?"

"To begin with. One titular wife ... The rest will just be my concubines."

I was at a loss as to whether I should absolve, envy, congratulate ...

"It was indispensable for my job at the Ministry," he explained, "and in particular for my business contracts . . ."

I was impressed. Who knows! My neighbor seems to be well on the way to fathoming the Chinese. He will go far! He must already know quite a number of ins and outs . . . I was about to . . .

. . . when there was a knock at the door. Time for my lesson with the Belgian. The boy showed him in quite naturally and straightforwardly, and then asked as an afterthought if the "foreign professor" might come in. Of course! Nothing could be simpler than to introduce in passing . . . Mr. . . . . Oh dear, I found I had omitted to register my "little Belgian's" exact name —what was it, for heaven's sake, his surname, his grocer's name! I mumbled something and concluded, "Professor at the College of Nobles." Then, stealing a glance at the European verso of the other's visiting-card, "Mr. . . . Mr. Jarignoux, clerk at the Ministry of Communications."

And two thoroughly different characters they were! The young Belgian, despite his ancestry, is slim and dark, with a curious, matte complexion; he barely condescended to rest his eyes—and they are extremely handsome eyes—on the man from the Ministry, who is short, fat, fair, lively, and pink, for all the forty-five years written in his jowls and wrinkles. They shook hands and passed one another by. As I was showing Jarignoux out with suitable pomp, he turned to me and said, indicating the Belgian, "Do you know that boy?"

"Do you, then?"

"Me? Oh no, I don't know him at all."

And he said he would call again for another neighborly chat, promising to assist me in my efforts to "understand" the Chinese.

The twin leaves of the door closed behind him with a click of their copper latches. I went back to my Belgian and asked in my turn, "Tell me, have you met that gentleman before?"

"Yes, I've seen him at father's, I think." He added, with

an expression of chaste repugnance that was not unamusing on his young and well-formed lips, "They say he has Chinese women."

"And?"

"Shall we begin our lesson?"

"Indeed . . . Yes . . . It's true, though. He was telling me of his recent marriage. But it's just struck me—how on earth can a European legally 'marry' a Chinese woman? I thought it was forbidden . . ."

Looking up from the text to which he was devoting a rather excessive amount of attention, my tutor assumed a look of scorn far too serious for his youthful features.

"Yes, but he is 'Chinese.' "

"Oh my dear man, you can't have . . . Didn't you see him? Reddish brown hair, round, gray eyes . . . and that accent! And look at his name—Jarignoux! There's no mistaking that. Good heavens, it positively reeks of Picardy!"

My tutor's scorn became even more marked.

"He is not a European any longer. He is a naturalized Chinese and has been for two and a half months, almost exactly— he had to have his ten years' residence."

So intense was my tutor's disapprobation that I restrained my curiosity. He is a long way from "fathoming" the Chinese, from having his hand on the pulse of China! I suggested as much to him.

"And has that course never tempted you? Speaking Pekingese as well as you do, you could . . ."

"Me?"

His eyes flared.

"Me? No—never!"

He turned to our lesson, and perforce drew me with him.

The characters would not stay still. My mind was elsewhere. I was thinking that, in China, full and complete naturalization was very likely accompanied by serious drawbacks. The first thing that struck me is what one would lose—those prerogatives which the foreigner enjoys here and with which it is best not to interfere . . . Naturalized, one would come under Chinese law and be liable to be denounced, dismissed, dissected, and dispatched with a speed and adroitness unknown to European judicial procedure. Instances of injustice are no more common . . . but distinctly more irreparable. There is the cangue, too— an unpleasant method of torture which I have seen well described in the illustrated press of the West.

Never mind—let us think only of what he gains from his renunciation . . . and what I gain myself. Mr. Jarignoux is my neighbor and a Chinese citizen. I can thus, while avoiding his vicissitudes, enjoy a share (perhaps) of his winnings. He will tell me things. He will introduce me to his new fellow-citizens —and they will introduce me to important officials, advisers to the throne . . . Princes of the Blood . . . The Palace is definitely becoming more accessible.

But meanwhile the columns of characters ranged so neatly down the page persisted in their refusal to stay still and even began to show signs of growing impatience. I had stopped listening to the monotonous commentary in the monotonous Belgian voice. I had lost interest. I was thinking that there was a good two hours' daylight left.

I decided I would go out and, for the umpteenth time, trace and as it were renew contact with that square of walls to which I shall one day, one way or another, be granted admittance . . . I am convinced of it.

"I have a slight headache," I said in dismissing my tutor. "I think I'll go out and get some fresh air over by the Observatory . . . There's a little wooded spot tucked away in the southeastern corner of the Tatar City which is absolutely . . . You've never come across it?"

"No, I must go home. My father needs me early today."

I left him with a feeling of relief—the dutiful son of a truly excellent grocer.

Moreover I promptly turned my back on the Observatory and the "southeastern corner" and headed my horse at a fast trot in the direction of my true objective—the Imperial City, which contains the purple-walled Forbidden City, the Within. It is perhaps the twentieth time I have set out thus to lay siege to the place, encompass it, verify its exact contours, circle like the sun about the foot of its eastern, southern, and western walls, and try if possible to complete the circle and come back by way of the north.

I avoided the "Street of the Legations"; it is too clean and its surface too hard for my horse's hoofs. Cutting west across the magnetic and imperial axis I passed the dynastic gate of the Palace, Ta Tsing Men, the "Gate of Supreme Purity," on my right. My glance was suitably respectful; threefold, squat, painted the same purple ochre as the walls of the Forbidden City, with large, leprous spots of gray, it is thrice closed to me. On my left, its towering roofs bearing down on me, was Cheng Yang Men, the "Gate that faces due South," known familiarly to the populace as "Chien Men," its tunneled passage marking the point of transition between two worlds—the outer "Chien Men Wai," the Chinese Empire with its pleasures, amorous tributes, and junketings, and the other, the encircled, walled, confined "Chien Men Nei," the Inner City with, in the middle, the Within. After a moment spent poised between cloistered virtue on my right and gaping vice on my left, I eluded both and rode on. Making my pensive way through crowds of people who for their part showed great nimbleness in eluding my horse's hoofs, I began my tour of the wall, keeping it always on my right.

Towards the west it is slightly disconcerting. Having to follow the line of the lakes, it lacks the four-square solidity of the eastern side. Its recesses betray the outline of the gardens it protects. The tops of trees protrude above its crest, and one can see a frieze of glazed roofs gleaming blue and yellow . . . Gazing intently about me, I let my horse follow the line of the moat.

My attention was attracted by a tall Chinese building to my left—paradoxically tall, I thought, for a building that stood so close to the Palace, from which indeed only the road separated it. On the lintel above the doorway I recognized an inscription in bold Arabic characters. This was a mosque.

And I remembered that, for good or ill, and notwithstanding all the reciprocal slaughters and persecutions of history, twenty million Moslem subjects have recently and forcibly been rallied to the Empire.

Curious how that mosque overlooks the wall . . . There it stands, an unrelenting yet unchastised observer, daring day and night to look where my eyes yearn to follow, namely *over the wall* . . .

Turning at right-angles to my right, I urged my horse to a gallop up the long, dusty road that runs northward in a straight line parallel to the wall. The Hsi Hwa Gate in the distance grew larger with each stride of my horse without there being any further change in my surroundings, so uniform is the wall there for a good thousand paces.

Dropping to a walk, I turned eastward through the gate and entered the Imperial City, home of the first conquerors and now open to all . . . but close, with only one last wall between them, to the Palace, the Within, the "Middle" . . . Indeed, above the crest of that wall, great gray and yellow and blue buildings reared up and suffered themselves to be seen—the ridges of temple roofs, two-storied palaces, and the bulbous mass of the "White Tower" thrusting out its alien paunch like a Buddhist stupa, imposing its Hindu personality . . . And a newcomer, at that! In the presence of four thousand years of Chinese "Ages" and the authentic cult of "Heaven," both its shape and the piety that inflates it really do seem a little . . . *art nouveau*.

Moreover, it irritates me. It is an alien presence in the Palace. Worse—an infidel presence! It ought not to be there! Such were my thoughts as, turning in the saddle and keeping it in sight, I continued around the long, meandering line of walls of which it forms the center. I gave my horse its head. The road was free, and besides I was the only European about. The Chinese would get their barrows out of the way.

The White Tower had disappeared when, my horse having pricked up its ears, I reined in. Ten paces ahead of us was another rider—also European—in difficulties with his mount.

The animal was prancing about and stamping its hoofs in the middle of the road, though this was quite deserted. It looked like a spirited beast, but I could see nothing that might have frightened it . . . I therefore diagnosed a nervous rider. Indeed the latter, instead of calming his mount, was behaving in a manner that defied all reason, looking about him at the walls, inspecting them closely, and then glancing along a parapet to his right. (The road passes over an embankment at that point, forming a hump.) Eventually he looked up in my direction—and with a start I recognized my tutor.

He had caught me on the hop, I realized. The Observatory and the "Corner Pavilion" were all of a league away—and in the diametrically opposite direction to the place of our meeting! But then what about himself?

He greeted me in a most courteous fashion, showing neither surprise nor embarrassment. His horse had abruptly recovered itself and fell into step beside mine as naturally as if they had been heading for the same stable.

Rather at a loss, I said, "You didn't tell me you rode."

"Oh, I just exercise my father's horses."

"That one seems a little highly strung . . . ?"

"He's scared of everything. He's thrown me eight times."

"Why do you ride him?"

"He's the most fun . . ."

Just then his horse circled and threw itself first on my own mount and then on myself, its lips drawn back over a quite ferocious set of teeth . . . It slipped—very fortunately—on a stone, executed a pair of caprioles, received a royal thrashing, and eventually, still snorting, consented to stand still. I was very much shaken up. My tutor, holding himself stiffly in the saddle, began to apologize for his beast's behavior . . .

"Did you notice," I interrupted, "how the road sounded hollow there?"

"No . . . Oh yes, possibly . . . One of the Palace drains . . ."

"A drain? Or could it be an aqueduct? Where does the water from the three lakes enter the Palace, in fact?"

He did not know. He knew nothing of the Palace, he said, beyond what little "everyone" knew—the outside, the rough-cast walls. I suggested we return together.

"Round by the north?"

"Certainly. If one can."

I had become inextricably lost on a couple of occasions, trying to find a way round the bottom of the ramparts.

"One can. Allow me . . ."

He went ahead and plunged into a maze of little side streets. I found we were following the wall very closely, if intermittently. We would lose it, then find it again; leave it for a while, then rejoin it across stretches of waste ground littered with dung-heaps and children. What I had taken to be the uniformly rectangular courses of this gigantic chessboard of a city began, as we rode on, to assume the quality of a "knight's progress."

My tutor set a good pace, slowing down exactly where necessary to take the narrow turnings at a brisk trot. I am certain that our route followed the line of the Great Forbidden Wall very closely—much more closely than I have ever dared attempt on my own. In places one could virtually touch the wall across the narrow moat. Eventually we came out to the north of the Palace.

The place was familiar to me, but from quite another approach—along the main carriageable avenues! I wondered whether I should recognize it. Yes, there was "Coal Hill"—we should be passing between it and the complex of buildings constituting the Palace itself.

Pointing up at this mound with its five crowning kiosks, my tutor said, "It's absurd—all the Europeans call it 'Coal Hill.' "

"Well?" I asked.

"Well, it's ridiculous. The proper name is 'The Hill of Contemplation.' "

I gave the—possibly artificial—mamelon an appraising look, with its five extremely elegant kiosks catching a few last, lingering rays of sunlight, and said regretfully, "Of course. From the top one must be able to 'contemplate' the entire Tatar City, the Chinese City, even . . . and as for the Palace, one would look right down into it as if . . ."

"No," my tutor flatly interjected. "The roof of Kien Tsi Tien is in the way."

I looked at him. His expression was unchanged. And yet he knew that inside the Palace there was a Kien Tsi Tien the roof of which, viewed from up there, cut off one's horizon to the south. It must mean . . .

"Have you been up there? Can one go up there?"

"No," he replied. "I know from one of my pupils, a nephew of Prince Lang."

"Oh, you teach the nephews of princes?"

"Naturally—at the 'College of Nobles.' "

He was gathering his reins. I stopped him.

"Let's stay at a walk. I want to take a look at the Palace over the ramparts."

I stood up in the stirrups. The Palace moat was full to the brim, like a pool after rain, with sluggish water thick with silt and sap, leaden water whose bland surface, pregnant with depth, laboriously bore the large, round, pale-green leaves of the Palace lotus, now just on the point of blooming . . . Not a ripple disturbed the reflection of the yellow-roofed pavilions, and I could count, upside-down in the water, the teeth of their two-tiered crenellations . . . All this motionless mass, this twilight moment that on me weighed so oppressively, the water bore without a tremor . . .

My tutor was waiting for me a little farther on, motionless too, polite—and utterly insensitive to the astonishing beauty of the hour. Unaware that those reflections in the viscous water, those hints of things sprung from the unplumbed depths of the ooze were quite deliberate manifestations of the justice of heaven, designed to represent both the secret beauty of the Within and the impossibility of looking upon it. All those passions immured, those dynastic lives . . . of which it seems unlikely I shall ever know more than I knew in that moment of that sloughy pond, *viz* the mere revelation of its flowers . . . with a fetid bubble or two . . .

Yet I felt a need to confide in someone. The hour lay heavy upon me, and he was there. After all, the young man had very pertinently given me the name of the hill from whose summit one may contemplate . . . I rode up to him. Indicating with a glance the Palace, the moat, the stagnant water, the evening, the magic of the hour . . . I told him all.

He heard me through without interruption, even where I touched on certain little-known details regarding the life of that noble, gentle prisoner of Empire, the reigning sovereign of the Kuang Hsu period. I told him all I know—the mystery of it . . . all the conjectures . . . those I have made myself, stretching to the limits of logic the marvels contained within those nearby walls, at the heart of the Purple City . . .

Nor did he, when I had finished, come out with any stupid remarks. For example, he did not say, "The true facts about his death were all in the papers at the time . . ." I was grateful to him. He had repaid my unexpected confidence with silence. It was a very good sign.

"My one great regret," I added after a pause, "is to have arrived in China too late. Every day I rub shoulders with people who were actually in there for the space of an audience and were able to catch a glimpse of him. Yet I doubt whether they were really in a position to *see*."

"I saw him," said my tutor, his voice suddenly full of respect . . .

A further pause. I urged my horse forward again. The animals had scented home and began to pull at the reins. We were no longer able to ride abreast, and in fact it required all our skill to dodge the enormous lanterns that swung down almost to the ground between the wheels of the mule-carts. Yet my companion insisted on forcing the pace to a degree which, in view of the darkness and the many obstacles in our path, bordered on the foolhardy . . . It was in a complete daze that I finally pulled up beside his horse—from which he had already dismounted—in front of a garishly lighted shop.

"Oh dear, I'm late! Father was expecting me back ages ago. Will you come in and take a cup of a Pei-king tea such as you have certainly never drunk in your life before?"

Realizing that he wished to cover his lateness with my presence, I accepted. Besides, I wanted to see his face again in the light . . .

We stepped inside. Ludicrous European interior. Yet he was clearly at home there. The father even appeared in person, "received" me, bade me be seated, and thanked me for being so good as to keep an eye on "this wicked devil," as he referred to his son. I drank his tea—which was indeed remarkable—and thought only of how I could get away, for in the light of that sanctum of commerce my tutor had abruptly resumed his homely, "fireside" look . . .

It was just too ghastly, the whole thing. A Dresden "Cupid" stretched out its arms towards a bunch of flowers so everlasting as to engender suspicion regarding their authenticity. The tea service was from Satsuma, *via* Hamburg. Not a suggestion, even a clumsy one, of the beautiful things of China, which, willy-nilly, are all about one here.

And yet . . . those two porcelain basins, exiles in that house, standing by the front door as if discarded . . . there was a sample of the real China, and a very fine sample too, even if they were recent (for I recognized on the cartouche the seal of the imperial kiln, "great dynasty of Ch'ing, Kuang Hsu period," on a yellow background with dragons rampant). What could those deserters from the Within be doing, I wondered, at the brink of that molasses barrel, on the threshold of that empire of preserves and spices?

"Yes," said my tutor. Showing me out, he had followed the direction of my lingering gaze and now replied to my astonishment, "Yes, they come from *there*."

Then, condescending to use Chinese for the first time outside the hours for which I pay him, he elaborated, "They come from the Palace, from the 'Ta Nei.' "

He accompanied me as far as the pavement, bare-headed and bowing at every step, and added in the same style, "Forgive me for not coming any farther."

Turning to give him the Chinese farewell, I noticed above his head the illuminated sign-board of the shop with the paternal name: "Import and Export, Leys & Co."

I remembered then—his name is "Leys." In fact, I even recalled his first name, "René."

That's it. My tutor's name is René Leys.

The brightness of day, shining gently opalescent through the opaque paper of my windowless and so softly luminous house, stripped me and washed me of my dreams of yesterday. The brightness of day . . . seeming, this morning, even further removed from yesterday and last night than it is strictly incumbent upon a tomorrow to be. And upon the brightness of this day, like a draught without bitterness, burst the rapid and fluent delivery of good Master Wang—at precisely the same time as on any other day. Nothing, then, had changed.

To work . . . for I must make up for lost time. Today I was determined not to waste a second.

"Master Wang, today I should like to learn the titles and duties of the inhabitants of the Within."

In defiance of all custom I had adopted the direct approach where it is common knowledge one ought to be circuitous.

Master Wang followed my example. In the same tone as he uses to enumerate the "Eighteen Provinces of the Empire," the "Five Connections," or the "Thirty-six Obligatory Virtues," he began to recite, "In the Within there lives the Emperor, whose honorary title is 'Son of Heaven' and whose title for the obtaining of a favor is 'Lord of the Ten Thousand Ages.' "

Fine. I got it down. Characters, romanization, translation. Next?

"Next comes the Empress, whose literary title is 'Middle Palace.' When there are two Empresses of equal rank at the same time, one is called 'Eastern Palace' and the other is called 'Western Palace.' The honorary title in both cases is 'Mother of the Empire.' "

"Excellent. And below the Empress or Empresses?"

"There are the Imperial Concubines—of the First Class, and below of the Second Class, and below . . ."

". . . Of the Third Class. Fine." I found these mathematical formalities held few enigmas. "Going down to number . . . ?"

The scrupulous Wang, wishing to leave nothing out, set off again from four to come to a halt at five.

"And below them?"

"There are the Emperor's Ladies of Honor. These may eventually be promoted to the rank of Concubines of the Fifth Class, who may reach the rank of Concubines of the Fourth Class, who may . . ."

"Yes, yes. Very good."

All his answers were straightforward and clear—almost too clear. He dodged none of my questions. He seemed to be hiding nothing from me. He spoke like a clerk, telling me the names of his colleagues—deputy chiefs whose jobs he had his eye on, "principals" who would "recommend" him . . .

It was thus that I learned, in due order and in the same methodical tones, the classification of the Imperial Princesses and of the Consorts of the said Princesses, then the colors— fields and borders—of the "Eight Banners," the complete heraldry of the Manchu conquerors, and this lovely title: "Prince of the Iron Hat"!

Finally Master Wang mentioned a curious caste of whose origin and functions I was entirely ignorant. These are the "Pao Yi," the "Bondmen" . . . yet despite the servility of their name I immediately pictured them among the Conquerors. They are descended from the "Eight Banners." Their leader—chosen from their ranks, and himself a bondman—is a Prince.

Master Wang was good enough to elaborate. These people, Korean or Mongol serfs of the Manchus of old, were led by their masters to the conquest of the "Middle Flower." They conquered. Now they are masters in their turn, and noblemen.

And what nobility indeed, what stately bearing! For the Manchus appointed lords over their new Chinese underlings these men who had served them so well in time of trouble . . . At least I believe that is what Master Wang was saying.

I made careful notes: "Pao Yi—bondmen . . . Pao Yi ts'an-ling—Chief of the Pao Yi . . . Pao Yi tso-ling— . . ."

"Come in!"

Almost simultaneously with the boy, René Leys burst into the room. It had happened! My two tutors were face to face. No sooner had this unexpected guest appeared than old Wang was on his feet, flexing his knees and touching the floor with his right fist in a Manchu—not Chinese—greeting that was perfect in its easy gracefulness. The Belgian, even before he took the hand I offered him, acknowledged Wang's greeting in kind as if by instinct, and with the same courteous, relaxed grace. Then, abruptly, he murmured an apology. He seemed very upset about something; there were tears in his eyes . . . He stood there without saying another word . . .

I too embarked on an apology. Indicating Wang, I muttered something about the good man not being a titular professor but simply a . . . native . . . friend who had been . . . warmly recommended to me . . .

I concluded, "In fact I was just on the point of dismissing him for the day."

"No need," said René Leys. "He doesn't understand a word of French."

This was true, I reflected. Besides, the good man had of his own accord retired into a book.

"Oh dear," René Leys went on with real emotion in his voice. "Things are going very badly for me . . ."

I said nothing, waiting.

"Father wants to leave Pei-king."

I must say I had expected far worse—or far better.

"He says he has some urgent business to see to in France. He'll be gone four or five months."

"And how does this affect you?"

"I can't go with him."

Why not, I wondered. Then I understood—of course, his chair at the College of Nobles, his "job." I had forgotten that this schoolboy held a highly qualified post.

He had read my thoughts.

"No, it's not my professorship. It's father—he doesn't want me with him."

My immediate feeling was that the father was very wise! But the expression on the son's face appeared to reproach him with quite other matters. Through a veil of reticences (shyness, perhaps?—yes, because subsequently he spoke more at his ease) I pieced together such a tale as I was far from expecting. The grocer, I learned, was realizing all his assets, parting with the shop, the furniture, the building itself, everything, and had quite literally turfed his son out to fend for himself. Moreover this unprepossessing parent, this "thrifty" merchant had apparently gone so far as to say, "Now perhaps your Chinese will do something for you for once. You can go and rent a *yamen* in the Tatar City and entertain your friends there!"

"Do you have Chinese 'friends,' then?"

"*That*'s not what bothers me," René Leys admitted, blushing suddenly. "I mean, what am I to do? I've never lived on my own."

I looked at him. True—his actual age is seventeen or eighteen. His face and eyes, though . . . much older, somehow . . . It is hard to describe.

"Ah, you've never lived on your own?"

"I've never even spent the night anywhere but in my parents' house." He hesitated, then went on, "I don't like the idea one bit. I can't sleep . . ."

There was nothing I could do about that, any more than I could about his father going away.

"I'm afraid of what happened to me once as a boy happening again . . ."

"And what was that?"

René Leys avoided my glance.

"Being bitten. Father always laughs at me when . . . I don't discuss it with him any more. I was bitten in the finger one night—this finger."

"By whom?"

"By whom?" Then, in a different tone, lowering his voice, "Yes . . . who could it have been? I never thought about it. Anyway, I was bitten. I jumped out of bed. There was a ring at the door. I was alone. My parents had been away and I thought this was them coming back. It was before my mother died . . . I went to the door, opened it . . . and there was this enormous flame . . ."

"Then it was the flame that had rung," I said with a sarcastic chuckle. I have no time for these ghost stories. You can always tell what is going to happen, and you get twenty explanations—all of them false—thrown in.

But René Leys' glance as he looked up was misted with a quite genuine fear, and I realized that the lad had seen some pretty disturbing things—real or unreal—in his childhood. He sees the world through eyes quite different from my own, I thought. In fact I noticed just then that he was staring fixedly over my shoulder at something behind me . . . I itched to turn round.

Eventually I accepted—without either approval or congratulation—that he was afraid of being alone. And immediately I had an explanation of the change that came over his voice and manner as night fell . . . I became convinced that my tutor was no ordinary person. An idea then occurred to me that was full of practical curiosity. My Chinese house is enormous, consisting of a number of buildings distributed around a series of square courtyards . . . I could put a camp-bed in the southern pavilion. He could eat at my table, and I would have an excellent tutor virtually in attendance, as it were. Moreover, he had sufficient outside occupations to prevent him from being in my way.

And then . . . I felt drawn to the lad, very drawn to him all of a sudden, in spite of his awkwardnesses, his childishnesses, his groceries, his fears . . . So I offered him bed and board under my roof. And the thing was suggested, accepted, concluded, and arranged in less words that it takes to tell. Indeed, it was as if everything had been ordained in advance.

When he took his leave he said no more than he usually says. He is capable of reserve, then. That too is a good sign.

A stupid day. Master Wang, as if drained completely of all he had to tell me about the Palace, hemmed and hawed, repeated himself, dried up completely, and then went back to his catalogue of Functions and his inventory of Princesses, Concubines, and Ladies-in-Waiting. I had more than half a mind to ask him rudely about his wife's ordinal number at the Palace—thirty-third dishwasher or ninety-fifth groveler in expectation of employment?

I swallowed all my ill-feeling against my good neighbor Jarignoux. I really owed him the visit I paid him—in fact, this was the sole reason for my paying it, for I have been thinking about his case and am convinced he has played his cards very wrongly in becoming Chinese.

At least let him be useful, I thought. Affecting a guileless and slightly abstracted air, I brought up the subject of the young Belgian whom he so emphatically denied recognizing at my house the other day. Now, all of a sudden, it appeared he does know him. And well, too, because he immediately came out with a most damaging remark about him—though perhaps not, after all, saying so very much . . .

"A notorious libertine, sir!"

"Oh, for heaven's sake!"

I could still hear René Leys' artless voice telling me of his fears at sleeping away from home. And anyway, his reputation is his own business! I said as much to Jarignoux.

This appeared to upset my good neighbor. No doubt he had been expecting the classic rejoinder: "He's enjoying himself—only right at his age." Yes, I'm sure that's what he expected me to say! My silence suddenly made him turn moralist. This young libertine, he explained, had a father, and that father was a married man, now a widower! A person worthy of respect! And never would he (my neighbor), as a friend of that father, disclose some of the things he knew . . .

I let him disclose them. What they amounted to was this: René Leys is apparently an assiduous, in fact nightly frequenter of the "teahouses" of Chien Men Wai.

Jarignoux gave me a look. "You know what I'm talking about?"

"Chien Men Wai? Oh . . . I can imagine. But what of it?"

At this point my moralist changed his tune and began of his own accord to find excuses for the culprit he had so recently indicted.

René Leys, it appears, suffered a neglected childhood. He had the misfortune . . . (no one ever dares call it anything else) . . . he had the misfortune to lose his mother at an age when children usually only lose their milk-teeth. (So I shall never know whether this particular mother would have been worth keeping.) She was French. (This much is fact. Possibly from the Midi, which would account for the matte complexion and the big, beautiful eyes . . .) His father is a Walloon merchant. The boy was left rather to his own devices, that is to say he was sent to the *lycée* in Belgium where he succeeded in reaching one of the higher forms on the modern side. The paternal business then brought him to China, where he arrived at the age of fifteen to find himself suddenly lost and with time on his hands. It was for this reason alone that he took up Chinese which, one must admit (said Jarignoux), he speaks well.

(I would go further; I consider he has a quite extraordinary facility in handling the vocabulary of any and every language.)

Jarignoux, who does not appear to enjoy the same gift, stopped short, wondered whether he had not said too much about the young man, and then beat a retreat.

"After all, I don't know him myself. But the father, sir—there is a man for you!"

We went on to talk of other things. Not for very long. I no longer see my way to those "important officials" quite so clearly, and in fact my neighbor's and my paths may easily never cross again. But I have returned his visit. I have been polite.

I had been virtually counting on his coming. That is like me. (I confess to a pang of regret at seeing his empty place at table this first evening.) Then I hardly had time to have a bed set up for him . . . and there he was. But so late! I had given up expecting him.

Nothing has changed in the beauty of the night. As spring swells suddenly into summer I find myself spending most of my time in the largest of my internal courtyards. I dined out here beneath a square of darkening sky. Afterwards I read and wrote a bit, but mostly I lay back in my cane chair and gazed, without thinking of anything in particular, at the concave ceiling of the sky . . .

And there he was, suddenly beside me, and calm, as if the rectangle of my walls shielded and reassured him.

He sat down. I ought to have thought of something to say, obviously, but I said nothing. I enjoyed with him the feeling of security that the geometrical quietude of my house provides. Occasionally a cheese or noodle vendor went past in the street, uttering his extraordinary cry—an anguished modal note resolved by an astonishing and triumphant return to the exact tonic! (All to sell a bit of bean-cheese and a few greasy noodles!)

But his cry mingled with the scent of my barely open lotus

celebrating its own triumph over the cloudy water of the porcelain basin in the middle of my courtyard. It was one of those searching nights where everything fuses, dissolves, and disappears.

Still René Leys said nothing. What tact! What a sense of occasion! So it was for me to invade the silence and the darkness ... No, I continued my musing, and with even greater clarity and lucidity than the midday sun upon my rooftops. I meditated that, lying there with my head in this direction and my feet in that, so close to the southeastern corner of the Tatar City, I was lying exactly along a line from north to south. Like all the houses, palaces, and huts of Pei-king, my house, hut, or palace is very astronomically oriented (and occidented) with all its principal buildings facing south. Now it is one of the chief items of the Imperial code that "the Emperor be known as He Who Faces Toward the South." This gave me a sense of having no part whatever in the abject and "unanimous" life of the worms that wriggle and seethe on the dung-heap or the tapeworms that infest the gut but rather of living *a parallel existence*, in all the cold and measured rigorousness of the term, to the hidden life of the Palace, which like me "faced toward the south."

It struck me that it was time I asked René Leys to tell me how he had ever contrived to see "Himself," the former prisoner of the "Cardinal Palaces." Had he, I wondered, had an audience? Or had it been on the occasion of an imperial sacrifice at the Temple of Heaven (though I knew full well that the streets had always been sealed off)? Finally I voiced my thoughts aloud.

"You did say you saw Himself?"

René Leys stretched. I rather think I had woken him up ... that he had been sleeping peacefully for the last half hour ... Yet he replied without hesitation.

"Better than anyone." And in a quiet, gentle voice he went on, "I saw him, yes. I used to see him often, particularly mornings between ten and twelve. He was very alert then, very quick. He really applied himself to affairs of state . . . Afterwards he played with his women . . ."

"Really? But I'd heard . . ."

"He played innocent games with his women. For instance there was one game, a Chinese game, where you ran and tried to touch one another . . . or rather tried to avoid being touched . . . Each person had his place . . . As soon as he left it he could be . . . Oh, it was all very Chinese . . . And yet . . . I remember I used to play something very similar at my junior school in Termonde. We shouted 'Pax!' and then we weren't 'had' . . ."

"Did Himself shout too?"

"Oh no! He had a different method. But he tired very quickly and he never ran. When he was on the point of being caught, do you know what he would do?"

". . . ?"

"He'd sit down. Just like that. Anywhere."

". . ."

"And what happened then? All his women went down on their knees before him."

". . ."

"Of course. They had to. Do you think a single one of them would have dared to remain standing when the Emperor was seated—even if he'd just sat down anywhere?"

This was irrefutable. It bears the stamp of the eyewitness. If ever I should come to doubt René Leys' entrée to the Palace this scene, as he evoked it for me this evening, would, I am convinced, dispel that doubt as ridiculous.

The question came to my lips that always crops up on the subject of Himself. "His death, now . . . It . . ." But then I neatly turned it round. "Of course, everything that took place then, although it is only a few years ago, belongs to another age entirely. It's all over now. The Palace today is as tightly sealed as ever and inside is nothing but a great emptiness. It lacks grandeur. There are no 'successors,' no heirs. Nothing but shams . . .

'Highnesses' whose honorary title as far as I'm concerned, if ever I had to address them, would be not 'Your Excellency' but 'Your Supreme Inadequacy' . . . The Regent, for example, although a brother to Himself . . ."

René Leys suddenly became all ears.

"The Regent," I went on, "strikes me as a curious bird. To start with it sounds pretty feeble beside 'Throne'—the Regent! Yes, I know—there's the little four-year-old Emperor. Even less personality, though one has to allow for his age. But above all they had old Yuan! The cleverest—and strongest—of the lot! And they all but cut off his head! In fact he *is* dead . . . politically."

René Leys showed no reaction at my mention of Yuan, though he is well known among Europeans. Has he never heard of him?

"You see," I continued, "I arrived just three years too late. The old Empress was dead, after a sixty-year reign. So was Himself . . . having lived for thirty-four years . . . only. And could you even call it real living? I don't know. I don't wish to know . . ."

Indeed, I thought, it is extremely antiquarian of me to take such an interest in the Palace. It is already a "historical monument." It no longer contains a living reality. A few eunuchs, a few superannuated women . . . and occasionally, between two and four in the morning, the Grand Council with the Princes . . . rubbing their eyes . . .

Suddenly René Leys sat up.

"Oh, but the Regent! Don't speak of him in ignorance!" And again his voice took on that warm, velvety quality. "He is *almost* as intelligent as his brother, Himself, *'who has mounted the Dragon's car and gone to quench his thirst at the nine fountains.'*" (This was spoken respectfully, like a Chinese quotation.) "The Regent! But he desires only one thing—the happiness of his people! It is just that he is not sure how to go about it. He tries to study the people at close quarters. Sometimes he goes out completely unescorted. Once when he had spent the night in Chien Men Wai—Chien Men Wai is the 'district without the Chien Gate' . . ."

"Yes, I'm with you. Go on."

"The gate has to be shut at midnight. The fourth watch had just sounded . . ."

"Two in the morning European time . . ."

"Yes. I was with him. I haggled a bit with the gatekeeper and he let us through, both of us—in fact as Europeans . . . Next morning the gatekeeper woke up behind bars. You've got to have discipline. You can have no conception of what the Regent risks at four o'clock every single morning . . ."

"What? His reputation?"

"His life! Did you not know that at four o'clock every morning he goes from his residence to the Palace?"

"Ah yes, of course—to preside at the Grand Council."

"Do you know the bridge he goes across? Right in the north of the Tatar City, beyond the 'Posterior Gate' . . ."

"Heu Men—I know it well. The bridge is badly made-up and in any case virtually useless. I have never seen so many bridges spanning so little water as I have in China!"

"Wait for the great summer rains—June, July—and you'll see," René Leys assured me. "The whole 'Northern Lake' flows under it. At the moment, of course, it's dry. In fact that was what made the attempt on his life possible."

"Attempt on his life?"

And then I remembered reading in the papers the day before yesterday that "the Regent, driving from his residence to the Palace as he does every morning, had narrowly escaped being killed by a bomb which was to have exploded in his path." The abortive attempt had not made any particular impression on me. Besides, one is sated with so many juicier news items on the subject of the Emperors, Regents, Kings, Ministers, Parliamentarians, Presidents, and Queens of our European courts.

René Leys was surprised at my lack of interest.

"Do you know who discovered the thing?" he asked.

"No, I know nothing about it. No one knows anything

about it. I read in the papers that 'the police are investigating the matter and believe they have the people responsible.' So no one ever will know anything about it."

"The police?" René Leys pronounced the word with a quite Parisian scorn. "The police arrived . . . too late as well. It had already been discovered."

My ears pricked up a little at this. Was my tutor eventually going to make up his mind to tell me more than the papers had told me?

"It was discovered by Palace special agents."

"Do you mean there is a Secret Police?"

The ingenuousness of my interruption was affected. I know perfectly well that there is a Secret Police. Master Wang has told me. From his account it would appear to be harmless, ineffective, and extremely underpaid . . .

"And it was through them that the bomb was discovered?"

René Leys told me the whole story without further prompting. The bomb—an enormous affair capable of blowing up ten bridges all built of stone like the Heu Men bridge—had been fitted with electric wires leading . . . almost inside the Palace, to the foot of the wall around the lakes. Someone had spotted the wires, cut them, and then whistled—like . . .

And René Leys confidentially whistled a two-note figure exactly like that of our firemen at home when they go charging by to the rescue of some old lady, running people over right, left, and center as they go . . .

"That's the signal of the Secret Police, members of which were stationed at various points along the Regent's route. They came running and followed the wires, but they weren't quick enough to catch the person who was to make the contact."

"What happened then?"

"They detailed a coolie to remove the bomb and had it examined. Some of the parts were of Japanese make but the most dangerous screws came from an ironmonger here in Peiking . . ."

These details had certainly not been in the papers. Who had found out about the bomb and raised the alarm? I asked.

For a moment René Leys hesitated. It was so dark by then that I did not see him blush. I am sure he did blush, though.

"It was a . . . 'singing girl' from Chien Men Wai . . ."

And what was she doing at that matutine hour a good league north of her "precious lupanar"?

René Leys explained, point by point. She "too" was in the Secret Police. Hearing that an attempt was to be made on the Regent's life, she had stolen a march on her male colleagues . . . It was quite simple. And all of a sudden she had received, by order of high places, five thousand silver taels, having first revamped the somewhat antiquated furnishings of her room, which she had placed in a Chinese bank that paid her two per cent interest—per month.

"She sounds like a most domesticated woman. Might one perhaps . . . on a temporary basis?"

"Oh, not just anyone!" replied René Leys in his chaste manner. "But we could go 'there' together if you like."

"Why not this evening?"

"Out of the question," René Leys countered brusquely. "No, not this evening."

He did indeed seem tired, nervous, and unsure of himself. I would do well, I thought, to cut short the evening and send him off to bed—and go myself. But he would have none of it; he insisted that we remain as we were, lounging beneath the stars . . . The mood was still very confidential, and my mind soon resumed its vampiric prowlings about the person of my thrice-immured hero—immured, that is, by his life, by his dream, and by his death . . .

"Do tell me," I went on, "what was Himself like when he was alive? I've read so much nonsense about him. The editor of one local gazette described him as a 'languid, disillusioned Baudelarian.' I ask you!"

René Leys—who appears never to have heard of Baudelaire—replied in precise terms; his words were like touchstones of truth, embedding themselves in the black ground of the mosaic of the sky, the Heaven where reign the Regents who have passed away . . . One by one they drew the loveliest portrait that anyone will ever draw of "Him who reigned during the Kuang Hsu period" . . .

"A very intelligent, very gentle child with a man's years. The wisdom of an ancient who had forgotten his age. At times uniquely preoccupied with women . . . his women . . . princesses or attendants whom he summoned according to his liking or whom his aunt, the Aged Dowager—whom he called 'Venerable Mother'—prepared for him.

"Yes, deeply intelligent . . . very weakly, too, except during the first few hours of the day. He was fond of poetry, and had an elegant hand as he stroked 'with his brush-tip the tender paper.' " (This was enunciated in the rhythm of a Chinese quotation.) "He was fond of music, too . . ."

René Leys broke off, the word "music" clearly striking him as inadequate for what he wanted to express. But he could think of no other.

"Or rather . . . he loved to listen to anything that was brushed or touched . . . A gong that someone touched without actually hitting it . . . He would go faint with ecstasy! You had to hold him up. His voice a whisper, he would ask whoever it was to touch it again. And when the gong had stopped vibrating he would hear through the silence and burst into tears . . . I have seen him staring wordlessly at a drumskin . . ."

René Leys honored these memories with a melancholy silence. I could hear—just—the muffled iron and copper and tin voice of the "Great Bell" booming out the third watch far to the north, right at the heart of the ancient Mongol city now defunct . . .[5]

Its sound was hushed and noble, having passed over the roofs of the Palace, and come from far away.

"But he is dead," René Leys concluded.

"Yes." And then, coming back to it in spite of myself, "How did he die in fact?"

There was a pause. Was René Leys about to . . .

"Never mind how. He died without a friend beside him . . ."

It was true, I realized. In my . . . historical—yet how passionate!—curiosity I had overlooked this one point of which he now reminded me. The gentle, mournful child is dead—whether of poison or of dreaming, it matters little indeed. He died among eunuchs and women, with the terribly maternal eyes of the Imperial Beldam poised to mark his expiring gesture, and—the point I had overlooked—never a friend beside him!

René Leys had come out with the one thing that had been left unsaid.

"You're right," I resumed aloud. "But did Himself have any friends of his own—even just one?"

For there might have been one, I thought—a prince or a coachman, a clerk or a guard, someone who came up to the image of the great servants of old, serving Heaven in the person of its Son!

"Yes," said René Leys simply. "I was his friend."

And indeed, whenever a person like René Leys depicts another person in the colorful, true-to-life terms of the portrait that emerged from his words, it can only be out of the direst hatred or the deepest love. So René Leys loved with the love of youth that young and doleful Emperor, that castaway . . .

He looks very young and somewhat doleful himself when you see him no longer engaged in some physical activity. But how did he come to meet the Emperor, I wondered.

"Tell me—how did you meet him, your friend . . . How did you get into the Palace the first time? Who got you in there?"

I was not aware of being indiscreet. No admission could have been too solemn for the respect with which I should have received it. If I had understood rightly what had gone before, surely nothing could be out of place . . .

. . . except the dry, curt tone in which René Leys snubbed me:

"How did I get in? That's my business!"

All right. I did not press the matter. With difficulty I sup-
pressed an urge to send him packing. Did he think I wanted to
steal his dodge? I was preparing to retire, then, when there came
a knock at the outer gate—a Chinese hand was belaboring the
dangling copper handles as if they were hammers . . .

My gatekeeper failed to wake up. René Leys was on his
feet before me and I heard him parleying with someone outside.
By the time I arrived he had the gate open.

"It's for me," he said in the same curt tone, stuffing into
his pocket a pale silk handkerchief which I am sure had just
been handed to him. And, pausing only to pick up his hat (very
European, his hat—a "bowler," I believe), without a word to me
as to when or whether he would be back, off he went in the
large and splendid mule-drawn carriage that awaited him and,
the carriage negotiating a corner of the street, disappeared.

It is almost light. In the meticulous precision of insomnia
I complete these notes of a day which has disconcerted me to
the point of vexation—or pleased me very much better than all
that has gone before . . .

I could not sleep. At least, I was dozing fitfully in the broad daylight when my cook came in person—at the prearranged time, but this morning it seemed obscenely early—to remind me that I had "two guests" coming to dinner.

On trust I ordered something "well-balanced." And I recalled with an effort having invited Dame and Master Wang several days ago to grant me the honor of their presence at my table tonight.

This may have been bad form on my part. There is the famous saying—a Chinese never parades his wife in public . . . And I had even asked her to come to my house! But the fact remains that, with great ceremony, he accepted. I very much wanted a closer look at one of those glittering, decorative creatures whom one can pick out at quite a distance in the street as "a Manchu woman"—even one who had grown gray in the service (for I had not forgotten that she had been at court at the time of our Second Empire, nor that it was thanks to her underhand intrigues that her spouse had since held a post at the college of the Palace Secret Police!).

Also this morning I received the following undecipherable letter which my boy reeled off to me quite fluently: "Master

Wang, who lives in the very north of the Tatar City, begs to be excused if he only makes the journey to my house once today —for dinner." Fine, I thought, and went to sleep again.

Then, later in the morning, another note, written with the brush, but in Belgian this time, on wispy Chinese paper decorated with little pink and green flowers: René Leys begged to be excused—he would be unable to give me my afternoon lesson today. He would no doubt be back some time after midnight. His note ended, "I have been summoned . . . you know where."

I did not know. And I reflected that, for a lad who had never before left the shelter of the paternal roof, he was sleeping out with impressive regularity.

. . . Further sleep was impossible under that great yellow eye of the Pei-king sky—a sun so dependable day after day that one comes to claim it as one's due and to rely on it as on a faithful friend . . . So I took the example of my tutors and gave myself the day off . . .

And before that sun was casting a very much shorter shadow I was up and out and on my horse, en route for anywhere in the bright light that filled that immaculate dome of blue—"anywhere" meaning of course the environs of the Palace.

Guided by instinct, I found myself outside the Tung Hwa Men, The Gate of the Flowered East, which I was seeing for the first time at this princely hour . . . crowded with mule carts, flunkies, eunuchs, and officers in ceremonial dress—including their summer headgear, the conical straw hat with the red horsehair tail that is now compulsory. And dominating the scene was the massive, sloping flank of the purple, gray-flecked wall, pierced by the gate with its three curved copings . . . Again prompted by instinct, I knew it was about to open . . .

It swung open, and I was forced back by the throng that poured through it. I took up a position at the corner of the main avenue along which I was sure the procession would pass. The guards stationed every ten paces along the route hardly dared ask me—a European—to "move along." They did seem to want me to dismount, however, so I dismounted. With that I was left in peace, and after a certain amount of polite nudging my presence was accepted in the front row, where I was well placed to see . . .

Very well placed, in fact. This was the Grand Council coming out after its daily, pre-dawn meeting to decide what is to be done during the day. First to emerge is always the Regent, and as the gate swung back it was his escort that I saw bearing down on me at full tilt. In front came the Mongol pacers prominently displaying the standards. Following them . . . a most striking figure, a young horseman, swarthy of face, stocky, alert, his short legs exerting a powerful grip on the tall saddle with the high bow, the typical Chinese saddle on which the rider perches high above his horse's back . . . A piercing eye that took in street and passers-by with one sweep . . . Here, in a flash, was the whole victorious Tatar cavalcade at grips, two hundred and forty years ago, with a beaten China . . . Tough, nimble Manchus, wearing the long queue with which they tied their packs on their heads when they negotiated rivers hanging onto their horses' tails . . . Indeed, I thought, that sums it up! These were the conquerors, and since then hundreds of millions of Chinese have shaved their foreheads and drawn their hair back in a queue . . . without once crossing a river . . .

The conqueror, like the others, passed in the twinkling of an eye. And all Manchuria rode and as it were sallied forth with him.

All Manchuria . . . until the frightful European state coach through the windows of which I caught a glimpse of Prince Chun. So the son of the Seventh Prince and Regent of the Empire has gone European! He even has himself drawn by two enormous Russian trotters—and at a fast pace, I have to admit!

It occurred to me that after a couple more turnings he would be crossing the Heu Men bridge, the scene of the recent attempt on his life. If I leapt on my horse I could follow at a trot or even a canter along the lateral paths of the broad avenues of the city . . .

I was brought up short with my foot on the mounting-block, my attention arrested by a young Manchu officer riding behind the Regent. Slimly built, with a somewhat prominent nose and fine, dark eyes . . . I could have sworn I recognized René Leys . . . had not an oath to this effect been perfectly preposterous . . . The rider sped past me and was soon swallowed up among his companions. But my good René Leys will be highly amused when I let drop innocently that I have found his double in the Imperial Guard!

By the time I had finished staring after the double the procession was a long way off, the last riders disappearing in a confused rush. A new procession began—less swift, this one, but how much more classical! A palanquin borne by eight chairmen, and inside the broad silhouette of Grand Councillor Na Tung, "First Protector" . . . He was a truly fine sight, thus enthroned and powerful, but difficult to follow on horseback, the pace maintained by his chairmen being too slow for a trot and too fast for a walk. In any case I could not see any bombs going off under that fat and inoffensive personage.

So I came home again and eventually dropped off to sleep, waking to find it was getting late and . . . I had no flowers! One ought surely to have flowers when entertaining a young Manchu woman, I thought—for I had learned an hour before, through the good offices of my boy, that the present Mrs. Wang, far from dating back to our Second Empire (I am paraphrasing), was in fact Mrs. Wang III, and a woman of my own age . . .

In the end it was too late (one does not wait till dark to dine in China). I still had no flowers, but my hesitations were cut short by the arrival of my guests . . .

. . . A sight I shall never forget. "Mrs. Wang III" advanced towards me on high white soles three inches thick, balancing a tall, slender body surmounted by a face which I took in at one admiring glance and which shall form the highlight of my portrait: an oval moon, whited with makeup, divided by the obligatory long slits of eyes, and the cheekbones dabbed with two glorious discs of the most fatal ruby red. Her hair, glossy and drawn tightly back, was of the celebrated blackness of the raven's wing—which is in fact blue. It was taken up behind and held by a broad silver clasp. And her neck, it goes without saying, had the "oily polish of refined and moulded tallow . . ." (Book of Verses, Ode the Ten-thousandth . . .).

No, but I am ten thousand times a fool to mock myself thus. That face, scraped right down, would reveal an agreeable expanse of faultless skin, and beneath the straight Manchu dress, shoulders and hips moved with a nubile grace . . . Truly a most pleasant change from the plumpness of form and insufficiency of height that northern Chinese beauty tends rather to overdo . . .

Naturally I kept these various sentiments to myself. I went through the Manchu gestures I had learned from the husband the day before. He was proud to bring his wife to a "European Evening." She derived great amusement from my forks with their four prongs, from my knives and glasses—and from seeing the plates changed so many times for so few courses. But she was very taken with the awful champagne which father Leys of Leys & Co. sold me a month ago at prices that disarmed all further bidding.

My boy waited on us with a bad grace. He and I were the only ones aware of the indecency of this respectable woman's sitting there at the same table as her husband . . . even if it was a European table! But the lamp grew dim, robbing her colors of their glaring brightness. Her four-square hairstyle was lost in shadow . . . leaving only two eyes, now almost round, a nose . . . as it were modeled, and then those svelte shoulders beneath the supple, flimsy silk of her dress . . . One really comes to appreciate all the femininity of the flowing, immodest dress when one has seen the way the Chinese female encases her lower limbs in two sheaths fastened chastely at ankle and waist and proof against all desires—which she has in any case extinguished in advance.

Not forgetting, either, that the Manchu women do not hop about on a couple of tapered stumps but walk nobly erect with the foot laid flat upon a thick white sole . . .

Mrs. Wang, if my poor vocabulary comprised more floral and poetic words than your aged husband has so far taught me, rest assured that my first concern would be to essay them, unbeknown to him, at your feet.

Chancing to visit the southern wing of my house early this morning, I was surprised to find René Leys there, lying more or less fully dressed on his bed, fast asleep. He was very pale. I wondered what time he had come in, not having heard the gate open at all . . . but then I had been deep in dreams of Mrs. Wang . . .

I tiptoed out again and summoned the boy. He knew nothing about it but fell to insulting the second boy, who referred him to the coolie, who gave away the gatekeeper who had not been at his gate. Anyway, there it was—René Leys, having come in at some time during the night, was at last sleeping under my roof. Why had he not undressed? Was he too lazy, or too shy, or in too much of a hurry to be off again? I instructed my staff (and the order was immediately broadcast in a piercing yell) to make no noise during the morning . . .

"What—up already? So early? Where on earth are you off to now?"

"To take my class," replied René Leys with perfect naturalness as, washed, his tie in place, and a touch of pink in his matte cheeks, he emerged from his room and prepared to leave the house.

I dared not retain such a punctual professor, instead taking my irritation out on my servants. The gatekeeper, who returned in all innocence just at that point, swore that he had had to spend the night at home, mourning the death of his adoptive father.

I got little work done during the morning. I gazed out over my roofs with their elegantly curved corners and saw how summer was deepening the blue rectangle of Pei-king sky which is mine by right of tenancy. I looked at my lotus in the big porcelain basin in which there ought strictly to be fish with intricate markings swimming about. To kill time I tried to gauge the hour at a given moment from the course of my obliquely slanting shadow as it approached the axis of my principal buildings. And when the shadow cast by my body fell exactly along that axis I felt in my bones that this was the true noon at the meridian on which I live, on which I was situated at that moment as I sat on these paving stones, then saturated with light, in the quadrangular vat of this courtyard which is my Palace!

. . . And at that precise moment he came back again, but not alone this time: three young dandies accompanied him, whom he introduced as "Messrs. Ti Lang, Lang Ch'en, and Ngo Ko . . ."

Splendid, I thought. All Manchus. You can't go wrong with those two-character names.

He gave them my name too: "Mr. Sieh." Chosen from among the classical names of the "Hundred Families," this is the monosyllable that corresponds most nearly to my Western name—indeed my Far Western name, since it comes from Finistère, the "end of the earth"—my Breton name of "Segalen." The other two syllables go to make up my Chinese personal name. The whole is pronounced "Sieh Ko-lan" and pleases me not a little, because if I translate the "Ko-lan" part (leaving out the family name "Sieh") I get "orchid of the Virgin's Pavilion," which has given me new respect for my Breton "Ear of Rye."

The hour of their visit led me to believe that these young gentlemen intended to honor me with their presence at lunch. Unobtrusively I sent word to my cook to cater for "three extra guests at my table"—confident that a meal for five would appear in no time, for which I would later pay as if we had been a dozen.

While my "guests" chatted amongst themselves and pointed out to one another the indispensable European objects that have somehow found acceptance in my Chinese house, René Leys filled out the introductions.

"The big fellow there—the biggest one, looking through your library—works at the Ministry of Rites. The other one— the little fellow with the frown—is Prince Lang's nephew . . ."

"Ah yes, one of your pupils . . ."

"No, he's not my pupil. He's my friend."

"But you were telling me that one of your pupils was a 'nephew of Prince Lang.' "

René Leys gave me a pitying look and said in a precise voice, "Prince Lang has anything up to a dozen nephews. The one I teach is the eleventh. This is the sixth."

"I beg your pardon. And the third fellow over there—the one who is ruining one of my fountain pens by bearing down on it as if it were a Chinese brush?"

"*That?*"

René Leys put his lips to my ear and murmured respectfully, "That is the eldest son of Prince Kung!"

Here was something! This was precise. This was significant. The young man can demolish my entire desk, I said to myself, if he will only deign to do so! This is the eldest son of Prince Kung! And I went over in my mind, like an entry in some Chinese Almanach de Gotha, the marriages and the remarriages of the old Manchu who won fame fifty years ago with his negotiations—victorious in the midst of defeat—over the "smoking ruins of the Summer Palace" (from then on a historical monument). "Eldest Son" . . . he too historical. But what an astonishing disparity of ages between him and his father! This man looked that perpetual age—between twenty and thirty-five—of all Chinese and Manchus and Mongols who are not old men.

"I have brought my friends to see you," said René Leys in conclusion, "because there is nothing like multiple conversation for teaching one a language quickly, and in particular to arrange a further meeting with them this evening in Chien Men Wai—that is, if you can come . . ."

This evening? Right. It will make a poignant comparison, I thought, between my Manchu lady of yesterday and our prostitutes of this evening. We sat down to lunch. They talked among themselves in a stilted, artificial manner. The most incomprehensible of them all was René Leys, throwing out elegant witticisms and slipping in swift allusions.

Eventually my high-born young guests left me to go "back to business," apologizing profusely for having kept me from mine.

I can think of no better way of passing the time between lunch and the evening before me than by indulging in a lengthy contemplation of the city as a whole from its highest point. I shall ride to the north of the Tatar City and climb the ancestral Bell Tower, the "Chung Leu," that Mongol dowager of monuments . . . Looking due south over the white crenellations of the terrace I shall see the bulky "Ku Leu" or Drum Tower, the Hill of Contemplation, the distant, sealed-off Palace, the walls of the Tatar City forming a categorical, angular barrier . . . and beyond, farther to the south, the misshapen rectangle of the Chinese City, lying like a draught-ox at the feet of the City of the Conquerors . . . With a Founder's eye I shall trace the vast quadrilateral of which the Chinese City is but the southern suburb, the entire monumental concept dreamed by the Great Emperor "who reigned five hundred years ago, during the Yung Lo period," which proved too short for the completion of his wall! Within its fictive or actual confines I know that, from the top of the Bell Tower, I shall see the Northern Capital spread out before me over its plain like a mosaic in willow-green, yellow (the Palace roofs), and gray (the private houses).

I know that, if I then turn and repair to the shady side of the lofty monument, I shall be able to stretch out an arm and sound the great bronze bell with my fingertips . . . conjure forth for my ears alone its muffled voice of iron and copper and brass . . . that divides the watches as I shall have reapportioned the space spread out before me . . .

. . . And I also know that if I go on putting off having my pony saddled for the ride to the Bell Tower the sun will sink behind the "Western Hills" that stand guard six or seven leagues away over the plain . . . though in these days of the summer solstice it will still be light when I return . . .

I know in advance all that will happen and all that is . . . all that remains impossible. Why burden this manuscript with repetitions? Better to go out without constraint later, when day is done, to perfect the design—grown greater in the uncertain twilight of mere dream—in that inward moment that, turning upon itself, yet never repeats itself.

Later the same evening Yes, this must be the place, I decided. It was a restaurant; in front of it, a ceaseless coming and going of carters, scullions bearing various eatables, eunuchs bearing —alas—nothing any more . . .

Yet I hesitated. One does not just walk brazenly up to the "Palace of Earthly Delights"—as I deciphered the bold characters inscribed in black on the lantern . . . But then I saw him. René Leys came down a narrow passage to meet me and took me inside with him, behaving with simple dignity as if he were truly at home here.

A courtyard with interesting shadows and shafts of light . . . a large room . . . another courtyard . . . a "staircase"—actually an awkward ladder, but in any case unusual in a Chinese house, which is nearly always on one floor.

"We're dining in the 'Upper Pavilion,'" René Leys explained, "which is much more distinguished."

And there they all were. The word for "old friends" was already on my lips. I felt lighthearted and entirely at my ease among these young people of excellent family, who were clearly assembled with a view to "having a bit of fun." I looked forward to having some fun too—a lot of it. The Chinese can drink, there is no doubt about that. But the Manchu of noble descent, originating as he does from what is virtually Siberia, combines in this respect the skill of the Chinese with the imposing capacity of his Russian brother-in-law . . .

I recognized my lunchtime guests—the "Big Bespectacled Fellow," the "Little Nephew," the "Historical Eldest Son" . . . For so I had already baptized them, taking advantage of the right which friendship confers to bestow amicable nicknames upon one's new friends . . . But there was another person present . . . a striking and somehow familiar figure . . . Where had I seen him before? That flashing eye, those short, bowed legs seeking the saddle with every step . . . Beyond a doubt it was my "Tatar Conqueror," the vanguard of yesterday morning's procession. Here I was quite prepared for the introduction: "Mr. Chao, captain of the Regent's escort." Awkwardly he shook my thumb, forgetting in his ill-instructed enthusiasm to include the four fingers, which for a moment I was ashamed to see thus ostracized. But I forgave him. René Leys added quietly for my benefit, "A first-class officer, utterly loyal, very brave, deeply susceptible, and terrible in drink."

I did not doubt it—with that neck like a toad's and that forehead shaved almost as far back as the occiput . . . Oh indeed, I could picture behind him all of Manchuria swooping and thundering down from north to south, hot-tempered and yet loyal to the newly founded Empire! Good troopers, good archers, good swordsmen . . . first . . . intelligent . . . second . . . and terrible in . . .

Well, let him get drunk, was my feeling. And if in drink he becomes terrible and smashes a few glasses, I'm quite prepared to pay for them!

We were there to have fun, were we not?

But what was everyone waiting for?

Or rather "whom"—for, as René Leys explained, we were simply waiting for the Aged Uncle of the Little Nephew already present, in other words for "the uncle of Prince Lang's nephew." Splendid, I thought—for a brief calculation had led me to the conclusion that this meant the Prince himself—and it was with the most extreme gravity of bearing that I had myself introduced by René Leys to the old man who now appeared . . .

I brought it down a peg or two when it emerged that our "sixth" nephew of Prince Lang had as many uncles as the prince himself had nephews . . . This was "one of the other ones"—the fourth, or perhaps the twenty-fourth, it did not make a great deal of difference. At any rate, a nobleman of advanced age who had come along to have some fun with us.

Even better. There is nothing I like so much as to see old people enjoying themselves. The uncle appeared to be in the mood for dalliance. Hardly had we taken our places around two tables than the gallant ancient suggested we "ask a few singing girls round . . . to sing." This was fine with me: what more natural than that we should here prelude with music the kind of revels we induce so effectively at home with the dance?

René Leys, who seemed to be acting as host—and, to judge from his air of importance, as the one who pays, come the dessert course—asked for brush, ink, and a long sheet of red paper on which he proceeded to dash characters with careless elegance. This was a "correct" invitation, for it behooves, before visiting these ladies, to entertain them first in a place like the one we were in—and which was not at all what I thought I had read on the lantern outside. It was certainly a question of Earthly Delights, but I was mistaken as to the particular sense delighted here. This was the fourth, exclusively—the palate.

How long the wait seemed to me! The names he had written had been full of promise—"Jade of the Five Colors," "Tiny Sister," "Tested Patience," "Flowering Mountain," "Branch of Brussonetia Purpurea" (at least, that is the Latin version given by the Fathers of the Society of Jesus in their Sino-French lexicon) . . . And finally this unexpected and hardly professional appellation—"Indubitable Purity"!

How interminably long the wait began to seem! Neither the first, nor the second, nor even the tenth course that now lay on the tables succeeded in assuaging my thirst or taking my mind off the passing minutes. But at last—at long last—there they were!

What now? Was one supposed to choose . . . or was there to be a further wait? René Leys making no sign, I ventured to . . . He stopped me.

"Not that one! She's the 'fiancée' of the second son of Prince T'ai."

"Oh, I beg his pardon! Well . . . this one, perhaps?"

"Out of the question! That's Tiny Sister. She's the Aged Uncle's regular concubine."

I might have guessed! Tiny Sister, though, like the restaurant, offered palpable promises of truly Earthly Delights, but in a slightly different sense—namely the fifth . . .

At random I said, "The big girl there?"

"If you like," René Leys conceded, adding carelessly, "She's the policewoman I was telling you about—'Jade of the Five Colors.' "

I felt like going back on my choice. Love à la police was something I found disturbing to contemplate. I should be searched, stripped, and turned thoroughly inside out; I should be denounced, charged, and implicated in wanton and hideous crimes, when the very most I had in mind was an assault— against payment—upon the lady's decency!

In fact, I felt very much like going back on my choice. It was too late, however, I had already made myself plain, and the Belle of the Force was beside me.

I was immediately reassured. The meal proceeded in an almost domestic atmosphere and remained decent even by strict Chinese standards, with only the male guests eating and their temporary consorts waiting upon them. It was an excellent arrangement, for Policewoman of the Five Colors was very much handier with the chopsticks than I was myself. Besides, I loved this division of alimentary labor: I opened my mouth, she placed savory morsels delicately on my tongue, and I chewed and swallowed. I also did the drinking. In fact it occurred to me that I had already done a fair bit. The little cups—they were smaller than teacups—were kept filled with a tepid wine of the transparency of old *marc* . . . a rose wine, I was informed by René Leys, who drank little but urged me to keep drinking. I drank . . . I had, as I say, already drunk a fair bit.

I tried to study the faces of my fellow diners and their guests. The Aged Uncle was deep in conversation with his Tiny Sister, but—as René Leys remarked down the table—"they're talking business: he wants to buy her as his sixth concubine but they can't agree on a price."

Suddenly disgusted at this absence of sentimentality, I looked away—at the Aged Uncle's nephew, who was discreetly trying to prevent even a respectful glance from straying in his uncle's direction. The Big Bespectacled Fellow on his left had just come by Tested Patience. Chin up! I said to myself. Just wait! We shall see! I had the impression that, at the near corner of the table, Flowering Mountain was receiving the attentions of the Captain of the Escort, while Branch of Brussonetia, notwithstanding her name, was still unattached. Indubitable Purity, too, was free . . .

I made a sign to René Leys to the effect that he should abrogate one of these widowhoods. He barely acknowledged it. In fact nothing was further from his mind! He was entirely caught up in something quite different—namely a story which was being energetically narrated at the other table (the Captain of the Escort was clearly the hero of it for he was performing a terrifying mime of a man being sliced in two with a sword!). Had the culprit already been charged, convicted, disgraced, condemned to die at dawn, I wondered. On this very evening? Right away? In our presence?

"No, no!" René Leys assured me. "The captain of the escort was leading the Grand Council out this morning by the

Tung Hwa Men—the gate . . . you know it?—well, as he came out he spotted a dangerous-looking group of fellows stationed on the first corner behind the troop cordon. He had them moved along with the help of a few blows with the flat of the sword, but one of his men fell from his horse onto his own sword and cut himself in two . . ."

"Oh—only in two? Are you sure? And did you say this morning, at the corner by the Tung Hwa Men? But I was there! I didn't notice anything."

"Well, the others carried the body away, you see," René Leys explained. "The Regent himself didn't notice anything."

So I had missed an assassination of sorts! I ought to have followed at whatever pace. It was that wretched double who had held me up . . . Jokingly I congratulated René Leys on his new job: Grand Attendant in the Imperial Guard! I complimented him on the ease with which he sat on one of those Manchu ponies with the Chinese saddle, telling him I had promised myself to go and see the procession again one day . . . I expected some half-rude remark . . . a denial . . .

René Leys neither chaffed nor denied. Yet there was a distinct pause before he answered, "You won't see me in the procession again. I've just been appointed elsewhere."

And before I had had a chance to ask him what were his functions "elsewhere" he was deep in conversation again—with three people at once. Then he began to play the finger guessing game, exchanging a series of lightning gestures with the Historical Eldest Son . . . figures flying about like bids at an auction, eyes quick to seize the number shown so as to add just enough to make "ten." Loser takes a drink. René Leys won every time and drank little. I played pretty badly and drank a lot . . . How warm the rose wine seemed! And how lukewarm my courtesan, full of attentions but . . . of so demure a kind! How chaste were our revels! Such decorum . . .

When, I wondered, would it end?

In a room separated from our own by no more than a ramshackle partition there was quite another sort of commotion going on—a familiar one: corks popping, gusts of champagne laughter, remarks bawled in European voices of which the majority, if I was not mistaken, were French . . . Clearly a very different kind of party was in progress next door. I had thought my surroundings exclusively Chinese. And had it not been for the presence beside me, within reach, of the silk-sheathed limbs of my chosen courtesan, I could have sworn I caught an echo of a certain "Mont des Martyrs," of whom they celebrate nightly, far from here, the pagan . . . Parisian feast.[6]

"Yes, you're right," said René Leys, reading my thoughts. He had just obliged his opponent to "drain the cup" for the tenth time. "It's three or four French couples who wanted to try some Chinese food. The boys told me they brought their own supplies, including champagne."

"How boorish when they could be drinking this rose wine! No really, René—take it easy! This is my thirty-eighth cup . . . Oh well, *Kan-pei*, here's to you!"

I believe I did actually call him "René." I remember half expecting him to call me "Victor" in return.

"And who are they?" I continued imperturbably.

Not that it mattered. René Leys reeled off their names. I did not even listen . . . All I remember is that they were married couples. Heavily married. Well, by the beard of whoever invented matrimony, they certainly seemed to be enjoying themselves without let or lines!

I gave a passionate glance in the direction of my consort, my Constabular Beauty, my Provisionally Chosen, my pseudo-mistress . . . She was most definitely not enjoying herself, I thought. She was performing an honorable function entirely for my benefit. She must, I reflected, have spent most of the day asleep to be so naturally awake this evening. I scrupled to disturb a serenity so . . . professional. Yet what should she do at this point but consent to sit down—stiffly, and only just—on the furthermost point of my knee. Dare I, I wondered. From her feet to her waistband, nothing doing. From her neck with its high silk collar downward to her waist, not a hope. This left the waist itself, a chaste latitude, smooth and creamy to the touch, neither cool nor warm beneath the fashionable jacket with the straight flaps. With no great expectations I caressed the area. Abruptly its owner leapt to her feet in a state of high indignation . . . Clumsiness on my part, or was it trespass? No—my Policewoman was pointing accusingly at the partition, which consisted mainly of interstices . . . and indeed it became clear that we were being spied on at leisure by quantities of archly European eyes. We were providing a treat for the married women next door! Did they envy us? I thought it more likely they scorned us for our prudery, and for having made so little headway at this advanced hour . . . I had half a mind to render an eye for an eye. I was sure so much noise and so much laughter could not have been elicited without a measure of abandon. Well, they had my congratulations—I had achieved nothing at all!

Should I ask René Leys to come to my rescue, I wondered, but abandoned the idea when he got up from the table and drew Indubitable Purity to one side. I knew what his game was: he wanted to buy her—indubitably.

At last the meal was over. We had sampled the last soups in the approved fashion and rounded off with one or two grains of rice. We had wiped our faces with towels more damply warm than the round face of the Big Bespectacled Fellow, whose torso was bursting out of his flimsy jacket at several points.

That was it. René Leys politely informed me as to the amount of my bill, paying nothing himself (he told me he has a monthly slate of five or six silver taels at that restaurant), and we left. Our ladies elect now returned the compliment by inviting us back to their place. And that, I thought, is doubtless where it will happen, this eventuality which, in the Paradise of the Bestselling Novel, always happens sooner or later . . .

Nothing happened at all. Rather than keep anyone in suspense I prefer to get it off my chest: the sparsely-furnished hotel in which each of our ladies had a room would have knocked spots off any "school for the daughters of gentlewomen." Oh I know, I thought of that too—my Europeanness must have brought a blush of shame to their chaste yellow cheeks! But no one blushed, I am convinced of it, not even René Leys, who was very much at his ease and behaved with perfect good taste. Moreover, neither the Big Fellow, nor the Thirty-Sixth Nephew, nor the Eldest Son appeared to feel that our situation called for any other mode of speech or action than that of the most comradely unconstraint, or any other class of interlude than the frequent, unchecked comings and goings of other women come to visit "ours"—and of ours as they left us confidentially, to return . . . intact, hair unruffled, collars as high as ever, with neither a crease to their jackets nor a snag to their silken trousers.

Suddenly there were sounds of a scuffle down by the street door. The Captain of the Escort had already leapt professionally to his feet, red-faced and fiery-eyed, and was about to plunge into the fray . . . when René Leys, moving even more swiftly, barred the staircase, keeping him in the room, and went down himself to see what was going on . . .

The noise continued. We heard coolies abusing one another. Then there was a whistle, and clearly the last act of the drama was transferred to the local guard post.

"Just a fight," said René Leys, returning and exchanging a few hushed words in rapid Chinese with the others . . . "The thing is," he added in French for my benefit, "I had to stop the captain going out there . . . He would have been bound to kill someone!"

Then, with lowered voice: "And he'd have been recognized!"

"You don't say!" I told him. Was the Imperial Guard forbidden to visit "houses" of this sort, then? Or must its members observe strict chastity, like the Templars? If so, he'd come to the right place . . .

"No, no!" René Leys corrected me. "He'd have been recognized as a policeman! He's already got a record. And he's
terrible . . ."

". . . In drink. Yes, you were telling me."

He had just been drinking again. Taking a closer look at
him, I could sense the explosions going on inside this little man
who was all muscle and hard rotundities . . . He was playing a
long Chinese guitar with immense finesse, though he could more
easily have crushed it to dust in his fingers. And he was talking,
telling a story, gesticulating with eyes and cheeks without in-
terrupting the exquisite touch of his fingernails . . .

"How beautifully he plays!" said René Leys with an envi-
ous air. "He's noted for his delicate fingering. Do you understand what he's saying? No? It makes him furious even to think
about it. It happened here, in this room. It was in 1900, just after
the Siege of the Legations and the entry of the European troops
—he was sitting in this room one evening playing this same
pi-p'a when two fathead German officers, both much drunker
than he was, came in and started listening to him with tears in
their eyes. He stopped playing. They made a sign that he should
go on. Naturally he refused. One plays for oneself and one's
friends . . . not for Foreign Devils! Finally one of the *To Kuo-jen*
thrust the guitar into his hands by force and followed up with
a few punches to the head. With that . . ."

"Don't tell me. Built the way he is, he must have hurled
the pair of them through the window of this 'Two-storied Pavilion,' jumped down on top of them, and ground them to powder before anyone could salvage a scrap. Am I right?"

"No," said René Leys calmly. "With that he began to
play . . ."

". . . ?"

"They had revolvers. He began to play. Afterwards they
ordered him to dance . . ."

"And he danced? And then politely showed them both to
their carriage? I should have expected better of him."

"Ah, but he hadn't had enough to drink that day!" my friend René discreetly concluded . . .

Vexed, disillusioned, and disappointed, I hardly dared abuse the scanty rights vouchsafed me with dutiable graciousness by my pretty Policewoman or rather Customs Officer Elect . . . For one thing my vocabulary was just about exhausted. I really had nothing more to say to her. And I hardly liked to retain her in this state of inactivity when I could sense that, at every instant, her mind was on other things. Of the scene being enacted before me, all I could grasp was a few stealthy gestures. Everyone in the room, both men and women, gave the impression of being naturally about his or her business—but what business was it? Often they spoke in lowered tones. René Leys, half-reclining on an uncomfortable-looking bed, was devoting himself to Purity, almost whispering in her ear. The Aged Uncle had gone; the deal concluded, he had taken himself off with the Tiny Sister for whom he had paid such a handsome price (I believe I heard the figure of three thousand eight hundred taels mentioned, which at the current rate of exchange—three francs twelve sous—makes very nearly thirteen thousand seven hundred francs). Of course from now on she is his, commercially speaking, for life.

The Little Nephew had not followed his uncle. The Big Fellow was still sweating. I suddenly felt very lonely. Very disoccidented. The French laughter was far away. And there was precious little laughter where we were! Having already had rather more of this "hospitality" than I wanted, I had a strong desire to go home and forfeit the rest . . .

So I blessed René Leys when he came over and said, "Shall we go back to 'our' place?"

" 'Our' place? Yes, indeed—with the greatest pleasure. Where's the door?"

At last we were outside, just he and I, in the dark and

thrilling desert of those streets which, three or four hours previously, I had seen broiling with the light and heat of the latter part of the day. I was lost. I was terrified that I should never find my way. He led me safely homeward.

I tried to think of something to say. Had I enjoyed the evening? Shooting rather at random I offered René Leys my congratulations.

"I thought you were doing very well with Indubitable Purity . . . Tell me, it just occurs to me—why does she go by such an . . . improbable name, given her profession?"

"Oh, she's a virgin!" he protested with the greatest earnestness. "She's never been . . ."

. . . And here he used a delicately expressive Chinese verb, one which joins with the full bloom of the flower all the implicit defloration of still-tender sepals bursting asunder . . .

"Well what the hell is she doing there, then?"

I regretted my vulgarity as soon as I had spoken. But René Leys immediately proceeded to give me the background. This young woman, this "girl" (she is not yet fifteen, and in China a newborn infant counts as one year old), this virtuous child is Prince T'ai's second son's concubine-to-be. She lives in that house, withdrawn, "pure and close," as a very old song puts it, with her former school friends. (They are all literate.) From time to time she receives a visit from her Princely Protector. He for his part is very keen to bring this freshly-formed bud to red rose-hood—once and for all. She, however, demurs, wishing to remain as she is a while longer.

"Is the prince's son perhaps being difficult about the price?" I reasoned.

"No, it's not that," replied René Leys in that cutting tone which I am coming to know so well. "He is prepared to pay ten thousand silver taels—'ten thousand' is the same as saying 'infinity' in Chinese—but there it is—there's nothing he can do about it."

"But why?"

It was then that I was treated to this quite unforeseen, indeed unforeseeable remark: René Leys, eldest and only son of my grocer, Professor of Political Economy, replied with the utmost seriousness (nor did his listener burst out laughing at his words), "She resists his advances on *my* orders. He shall have her when *I* give the word."

It was delivered amid the vast solitude of the Tatar City's southern ramparts as we were at last approaching home. It was spoken in the tone of voice he almost invariably uses—a straightforward tone that simply expresses what is. There was nothing I could object to, no more I could ask.

The question that now hit me for the first time, and that haunted me all the rest of our silent way homeward, I asked of myself alone:

Who is this lad, this Belgian youth, who forbids Manchu princes possession of their future concubines? Who appoints himself guardian and protector of Chinese virginities and is not worsted by ten thousand taels of pure silver? Does he compete with money of his own? (But he has always struck me as extremely thrifty, and I know for a fact he has nothing apart from his salary, which he hands over *en bloc* to his father.) Or has he acquired some occult power over this naïve, pubescent girl . . . ? The few glimpses he has given me of his youth—premonitory visions, flames appearing at doors—indicate a highly-strung disposition, so possibly . . . No—Indubitable Purity strikes me as being in possession of positively amaranthine health of body and mind.

It is not money, then, and it is not occult charms. That leaves his own charms—and there is no denying that he is a good-looking fellow. Even men, who are given to jealousy on this point, have to admit it: a European woman would be wild about him. But a Chinese!

These amours between foreign women and the handsome stranger, though of course they are a classic and well-documented phenomenon (the love of the Black Queen for Solomon, of *L'Africaine* for Vasco da Gama, of all the rest for Loti), have never entirely convinced me, for they never go all the way— they never have children (not, at least, in the Bible, the opera, or the complete works of Pierre Loti).

And yet, for want of a better explanation, I have to assume that this is a case of love.

By the time I had reached this point in my reflections we were home.

"Well, good night, Leys. Sleep tight."

He looked to me as if he could hardly wait to get his head down. And indeed this is the first proper "night" he will have spent in my house.

16 JUNE 1911

Is it old Wang's masterly lessons, the influence of Dame Wang, the clarity of the young Belgian's precepts, or the inquisitive garrulity of "his" friends? Or is it the keen air, the scholarly exhalations of Pei-king . . . ? Anyway, the fact of the matter is that I am making progress with my Chinese (such a practical language: it does away with syntax by reducing all the rules to three) and have suddenly taken a fancy to the Written Style, discovering a whole architecture, even a whole philosophy, in the orderly arrangement of "Characters" . . . It means I can now begin to make proper use of my tutors—i.e. as mere lexicons, tools which may be either good or bad, talking, reciting machines . . . For example:

"Master Wang, the other day we dealt with what is *inside* the Palace. Today, perhaps, we might run through what we have *outside* the Palace."

Master Wang agreed and began to recite: "Outside the Palace there is the Empire. The Empire has its frontiers. Within those frontiers are eighteen provinces. Each province has a provincial capital, then prefectures of the first order, prefectures of the second order . . ."

"Yes, I see—like the Concubines . . . What a splendidly

organized Empire it is! I should have preferred something a little more unforeseen . . ."

Master Wang did not understand my timid attempt at translating "unforeseen" into Chinese. Perhaps the word does not exist, rather as we say there is no such thing as "impossible."

"There are the 'Secret Societies,' of course," Wang eventually admitted. "There are people who give money and attend meetings where they talk. They suggest that the Emperor should be a *Han-jen,* a Chinese. But it is a lost cause, and some of them find their way into prison and lose their heads as well."

Rather to see what would happen, I threw out, "There is also Yuan Shih-kai?"

Wang's reprimand was implicit in the abstracted air with which he received my query: "Yuan Shih-kai? He is a former government official. He is on leave." And he added confidentially, "He has a very bad leg."

This much I knew. Yuan Shih-kai is in very bad odor politically. His "bad leg" is an entirely literary device—a euphemism. Leg is here used as a rhetorical figure in place of "head." The head . . . that so important and yet, in the History of China —and of Mankind—so fragile organ . . . that pediculous calabash that just asks for the chopper, with a hole—the mouth— that simply clamors for poison to be poured down it!

But just try and translate that into Chinese wordplays!

I must have a word with René Leys about it in plain French . . .

At two o'clock, in he came, punctually for my lesson.

"Do you mind if we spend today making a list of the Political Parties of the Empire?"

René Leys gave me a look of considerable disdain. "Parties? Don't know of any. There is 'the Court,' the Manchu Dynasty, and . . . there are the Rebels . . ."

"Well, let's talk about the Rebels."

He answered perfunctorily and I learned nothing new

from what he said. The secret societies seem to consist of clubs rather like the Masonic lodges of England and America, combining the purely commercial interests of the Cantonese profiteers under the biblical trade name Jehovah Business & Co.

But all this I knew already. So I concentrated my inquiries on what is known as the "Revolutionary" movement of ideas, and particularly on the person of a certain traveler in gimcrack "Rights of Man" merchandise calling himself Sun Yat-sen.

René Leys was particularly scathing on his account—with my full approval: he could never express all the political, moral, aesthetic, and social evil I think of this barely eligible electioneer.

I had another question for him, though—the one I had put to Wang.

"What about Yuan Shih-kai? What do you make of him?"

He gave a smile. I waited. At length he deigned to reply. "Yuan Shih-kai . . . a creature of the Europeans!"

I thought this really a bit strong. Yuan, I told him, is anything but a puppet . . . which is precisely what interests me about him. Yuan is a Mandarin of the Old Order . . . He once wielded imperial powers . . . Yuan started his career as a pupil of Li Hung Chang . . . a master . . .

"You're too young, my dear Leys," I went on, "to have known Li Hung Chang . . . Later Yuan found himself on his own, separated from his master, in Seoul, in Korea, as Imperial Resident . . . Don't forget it was he who fired the first shot against the Japanese . . . That was some responsibility, that was! He had to defend Korea . . ."

"It was a mistake. We were beaten."

"We . . . My dear Leys—are you Chinese? Then in 1900, when he was Governor of Shantung, don't forget that he took up the cudgels for the Europeans . . ."

He did not answer. Had that been another "mistake," I wondered.

"I know that back in 1898 he had failed to take up the cudgels for the Emperor against the Aged Dowager, and I also know that when the Emperor and the Dowager died he very nearly . . . well, he was in fact condemned to death, but his sentence was commuted to enforced convalescence . . . and he retired to his estate in the country where he has been ever since. But do you know what he does there? How can a man of his ability, in good health, barely fifty years old—how can a man like that just accept . . . ?"

René Leys gave me that look again.

"Yuan is a figment of the European imagination. There are far more dangerous people here in Pei-king who have not retired to their country estates. They don't live in the provinces, unfortunately . . . nor in the Chinese City . . . nor in the Manchu City, nor in the Imperial City . . . They live in the Within."

"Oh, come now! You know very well there is no one in the Palace apart from women and eunuchs, and an Emperor of five or six years of age . . . an infant . . . with four thousand years of history behind him!"

It appeared that neither the Emperor, nor the eunuchs, nor the women had it in for the Regent but . . . "somebody."

"I thought the Regent enjoyed full rights of surveillance and interdiction over all public figures, whether Chinese or Manchu . . . What race is this person, incidentally?"

"Manchu," replied René Leys, "seeing that she lives in the Palace."

"Seeing that she . . . It's a woman, then?"

"Of course. The only male in the Palace is the Emperor."

"Well, my dear Leys, the Regent has one time-honored and discreet instrument of political security at his disposal. There are wells in the Palace, I take it?"

"How did you know?" he asked with a start.

"There are wells . . . as there are in all the plain around . . . The terrain is the same, and the water from the lakes would never be sufficient . . . Well then, why has this troublesome, you say even dangerous person not already been put out of harm's way at the bottom of some nice, deep, fresh-water well? I have seen some splendid ones at the Temple of Heaven—with an enormous lip, carved from a single block of marble, like a jade drum, or like a huge thumb ring such as archers use, placed carefully on its side, with the thousands of notches worn by the rope . . . the rope of the bucket—you know, the rope that disappears into the earth, plummeting down to where you can see a scrap of sky . . . And when you look up, your eye pierces the roof of the kiosk, too, through a hole of the same diameter as the thumb ring, and you expect to see, by a process of inverse reflection, the well shaft thrusting upward to where the water's surface is mirrored in the sky . . ."

I stopped. René Leys had paled. He was staring at me— or at something—out of eyes that themselves resembled two wells of darkness. He looked as if he were on the point of fainting with terror . . . I could hardly believe it was because of what I had been saying, for all that must surely have occurred to him already. I thought perhaps some childhood fear had suddenly recurred . . . Ought I to speak sharply to him? Or throw water in his face?

He relaxed then, and took up mechanically not what I had just been saying but what I had been saying before I had let drop the unfortunate word . . .

"The Regent has an instrument of security at his disposal . . . But the Regent knows nothing of this yet."

"What about his Secret Police?"

"Its means of action do not extend that far."

"What do you mean—'that far'?"

"As far as this person."

"Look, is this person inside the Palace—yes or no?"

"Yes."

It was said in that final tone which his voice contrives to take on sometimes and which disarms all doubts.

"But if the Police can do nothing, the Regent himself is in ignorance, and meanwhile the hail of bombs continues, I really see no way out."

"I have found one," said René Leys. He got to his feet, having recovered his neat, purposeful air. "Would you like to come to the theatre with me tomorrow? They're doing one of the great old plays. It's been on for a week. You'll see the grand finale. But before that there's a very modern piece of stage business ... that will explain ..."

"Fine. Till tomorrow, then. Or shall I see you this evening?"

"I'm not sure whether I shall be sleeping here this evening."

Indeed? And where *will* he be sleeping, then?

My first thought was: what the devil is that fellow doing here again?

"That fellow" was the Chinese civil servant Jarignoux. It struck me then that his double-sided visiting card now bore a wealth of new and even more important titles, and that it was probably to tell me about these that he had come.

I was wrong. He had come, he told me after a brisk apology, to give me news of Mr. Leys Sr., who, having once had the honor of entertaining me at his home, sent me his "best regards."

How delightful! But why, I wondered, should Leys Sr. have chosen as his go-between in Pei-king this coarse fellow who, barely a month before, had sworn he did not know Leys Jr. "at all"?

"His letter," the go-between went on, "contains some rather disturbing news. He has suddenly decided to get married again. Just like that—from one day to the next."

I was on the point of expressing my condolences . . . but Jarignoux left me no time.

"This is going to involve him," he continued, "in considerable expenditure, and he wants his son to continue sending money regularly. He is also worried that the good-for-nothing may be laying out excessive sums on women. He's quite right, too. Young Leys is a shocking profligate. He spends every night in Chien Men Wai . . ."

"Oh!"

"I assure you it's true, sir! He consorts with a crowd of Chinese ne'er-do-wells of his own age, he drinks, he keeps singing girls . . . That's where all his money goes!"

"Surely not!"

"You only know him in the daytime. A steady enough young man, wouldn't one think? A real professor, eh? Sir, if you knew the riotous life he leads from ten p.m. onwards!"

And Mr. Jarignoux, in the name of the grocer father, charged his words with all the grief and indignation he felt at such a malversation of funds. I had to say something.

"Mr. Jarignoux, do you mind if I ask you a rather indiscreet question? You were telling me the other day that you have married a number of women. How is your third wife—is she in good health?"

Jarignoux lost some of his assurance. Clearly his third wife was not too . . . I did not insist.

"Well," he rather awkwardly resumed, "the long and short of it is, young Leys is causing his father considerable anxiety and his father has asked me, sir, to ask you to . . . keep a bit of an eye on him . . ."

"Oh, come now! It's out of the question! René Leys is my tutor. I have nothing but respect for him. And anyway, why do you want this lad, who has organized himself a most honorable existence here, to burden himself with his family?"

There was an embarrassed silence. Jarignoux had evidently sweated out all he had come prepared to say. I had nothing to add myself, unless it was the (inexpressible) wish that he should make his future visits as infrequent as possible.

". . . By the way, if you wish to get in with the Chinese, I should tell you that I have just been decorated . . ." (You need it, I thought, but this too I left unexpressed.) ". . . by the Minister of Transport and Communications. The day before yesterday I was invested with the Order of the Double Dragon, fifth class."

Feeling a little like a dragon myself, I waited for him to take his leave, which eventually he did. But Lord, how long! (*Long* = Dragon, but you couldn't translate the pun into Chinese.)

It remains only for me to forget his visit and his disparaging remarks, which have by no means lessened my sympathy for Leys . . . Quite the contrary.

Same evening   He came back early this evening, as if anxious to justify himself . . . Or was it the promise of rain in this storm that is about to break?

I indicated his place opposite but he declined to join me at table . . . He had dined early, he said, with some new Manchu friends.

If so, he must have dined very badly, I thought. He looked thoroughly washed-out and there were dark rings under his eyes. I was certain he had been weeping not long before. He sat down. He said nothing. I contained my curiosity. When he opened his mouth to speak . . .

"Come under the veranda, old man," I forestalled him. "We can talk better there. It's going to come down in bucketfuls out here in the courtyard! I'll have the boy clear the table and we'll put the lamp at the other end to draw off the mosquitoes nicely . . . Here—you take the couch . . ."

He reclined on the couch. Still he said nothing. My black rectangle of sky was full of the strained commotion that heralds a storm. We were both aware of it, and I had spoken quietly for that reason.

He lay back like an exhausted child. He would have fallen asleep immediately had he not, I felt, been consumed with a desire to talk, presumably about his affairs with the Virgins of Chien Men Wai . . . I could see that all was by no means well with him.

At length he spoke.

"I had a letter today which has deeply distressed me."

Don't say the Virgins have taken to writing letters too, I thought.

"Father writes that he is getting married again . . ."

Of course. I had forgotten his father. The information I had already.

"What of it?" I asked him.

René Leys could see that I was not particularly over-whelmed by his news. To get me to share his emotion he began to tell me about his family in the same confidential voice that was opening doors into the Palace the other evening.

"Father's wrong to remarry! It's no secret whom he's marrying! She's a girl he met once at Leuven on a business trip. My mother was alive at the time . . ."

There would have seemed to me little to take offence at here had I not glimpsed this struggle going on in the young half-Belgian's heart: his mother had been French, and he himself had no wish to be Belgian. Possibly, I thought, this would stop him ever taking Chinese nationality like friend Jarignoux.

But my chief feeling was that this was his business and not mine. Above all, the private life of a widowed shopkeeper contemplating remarriage did not, this evening of all evenings, have the power to grip me. I suggested changing the subject.

"What distresses me," René Leys insisted, "is that fa-ther's letter contains reproaches about my way of life. I don't know who can have been writing to him! He accuses me of compromising my position at the University. He has no idea!"

Here we go, I thought.

"Father treats me like a little boy. I can't tell him what's just happened to me—he'd go around shouting it from the housetops! Father thinks that if I gave up my professorship I would be out of a job. I tell you, he has no idea!"

And suddenly, with the energetic simplicity of a child wiping its eyes with a dirty sleeve, René Leys was himself again. His voice became calm, precise, informative. The news he was unable to tell his father he had to tell someone, and he would tell it to me. It is quite something: this eighteen-year-old lad—twenty at most—this foreigner, this barbarian of a Belgian has this very day been appointed to a top job in the Pei-king Secret Police.

I was not entirely unprepared. It accounts for a good many things. But I could never have filled in the details.

Having suspected for some months that the Regent's life was in danger, he had taken upon himself, out of friendship for the brother of his friend, the late Emperor, the duty of ensuring its preservation. He had kept his ears open in the company of the nephews and sons of Princes and listened to what was being said among the eunuchs and women—particularly during the latter stages of meals at which the rose wine flowed freely. He had also had the idea of asking the singing girls to keep their ears open too. Then, the day before the attempted assassination at the Heu Men bridge, the Lovely Policewoman—whom I had held, at a distance, in my arms—had most pertinently revealed the existence of the bomb, and he, René Leys, after spending the whole night on watch, had cut the wires and saved the Regent.

I could appreciate how solid his "job" must be after this initial success. I complimented him. He went on to say that he had been encouraged by the result and that he intended to recruit more "policewomen" in the houses of Chien Men Wai. They were reliable, he felt. He paid them, and they obeyed instructions better than men. Indubitable Purity, for example, would continue to withhold herself from her adoring purchaser until she received permission to do otherwise.

What a bitter disappointment! No mysterious amours, then. Only—in all the strictness and indubitable probity of the term—a simple . . . delivery.

I learned, too, that the Regent's secret police constitutes a kind of Ministry, and a highly organized one at that with its own offices, officials, clerks, and lesser employees.

"And its own colleges?" I asked.

"Yes. How do you know?"

"I too have my police. Go on."

I also discovered how René Leys dresses when he is received by the Regent—as a "mandarin of the fourth grade."

"With or without decorations?"

What I wanted to know was, had he received an equivalent distinction to the one someone else I knew had received . . . namely the Chinese civil servant Jarignoux . . .

He did not understand.

"The Order of the Double Dragon," I suggested.

And how scornfully he said, "That? That's for Europeans. A Romanian sword swallower who entertained the Regent last month has just been awarded it . . . And another fellow, the Frenchman Jarignoux, whom the Chinese have treated like a coolie ever since he became naturalized . . ."

Clearly he is very well informed, and indeed I am becoming increasingly so myself. For instance I have found out how he spends some—in fact the greater part—of his nights: he spends them at the Central Bureau of the Secret Police (or, as he calls it familiarly, the "S.P.") going through the reports that pour in there from all sides, from every clique and *yamen*, and from every kitchen and porter's lodge of the European, American, and Nipponian Legations.

The staff are a mixed bag: in the higher ranks, important mandarins; at the bottom of the hierarchy, the stableboys and valets who, whenever they are given a letter to deliver, take it straight to the "Central Bureau" where it is skillfully opened (an extremely delicate operation since Chinese paper cannot be exposed to steam), entered, read, and copied, and from whence it proceeds with barely an hour's delay to its addressee, whose reply duly receives the same attention. Each of these honorable employees is required to submit a "monthly report," which he communicates to his immediate superior—the only one he knows—who passes it on to the head of the organization, of whose identity everyone is in ignorance . . .

It is methodically organized and well administered. It "stands to reason." I had attached small importance to the few words I had elicited from Mr. Wang on the subject, but now I felt a certain respect for the man. And for René Leys, who had so authoritatively explained all this to me, I conceived such an enthusiasm all of sudden, such an admiration as to be almost on the point of bursting with it, like the swollen cloud still making its insolent way across the night sky above us . . . It was hot and very dark. But what did I care at that moment! I could see my way clear at last. Here was light, an open door, a way in! Here was my promised entrée—the red wall, the yellow wall, the impenetrable purple wall had abruptly become delicate, diaphanous webs that I should pierce and pass through like child's play arrayed in gorgeous costumes . . . My confidence at that moment was unbounded. I should know all, I felt, see all . . .

Impulsively I congratulated him: "So you're quite at home in the Palace?"

I expected him to come out with the whole story then. No doubt he was present when the Grand Council was held at dawn every day? One could assume that at a word or a sign from him the eunuchs bowed to the floor?

But no. In fact, nothing of the sort. Apparently there are barriers *inside* the Palace which all the Regent's secret police —even the Regent himself—cannot penetrate!

"Don't penetrate them, then! Why should you have to?"

René Leys became inordinately serious.

"You see . . . *his* life is at stake, every day. We have to get to the source of the danger . . . And he has no idea . . ."

"Well, warn him!"

"I'm afraid to. I don't like to give him such a scare a second time . . . You didn't see the way he trembled . . . the look that came into his eyes when I told him next day that he 'could have been hurt.' It was the same face his brother used to make! When he found out that I was the one who had cut the wires he called me his 'friend.' His friend! Do you realize what that means?"

I did. The word took on a marvelous sonority in the mouth of one who may one day be my friend. He himself seemed in

that instant suddenly to grasp and accept the full meaning of
the word in all its resonance.

"Look—you are the Regent's friend, is that right?"

"Yes."

"Well, if you are afraid on his account of dangers you do
not like to tell him about, and since you already have one success behind you, go for the radical solution. Ask to have two
companies of the Imperial Guard for a night and surround the
parts of the Palace where these 'dangers' are entrenched . . . A
fire will break out that evening—the work of some jealous or
spiteful eunuch . . . who will be rewarded handsomely for his
pains. Only those you let through will escape. When it's all over
you throw some water on the buildings around to stop them
catching. You will have made short work of the 'dangers' that
scare him so, and you will be promoted to . . . I don't know what
—Supreme Chief of all the Police of the Eighteen Provinces and
Tributary Lands . . . Go to it, my dear Leys, and your fortune is
made!"

I am not sure myself whether I spoke in jest or in prophecy. I was aware only of somehow entering into the spirit of the
thing.

But . . .

Just then I happened to catch his eye . . . It silenced and
deeply confused me. I was almost alarmed myself at the fear I
saw written in every feature. He was staring at me . . . I could
not think what he could have to say to me. He was quite frightening to look at with his sunken eyes filling with a mounting
madness, his mouth tensed to speak . . . By the shaven forehead
of his friend the Regent, I thought, then let him speak. In the
name of Fo and the Dogs of Fo, let him say something—anything . . .

He said, "No one . . . would dare. Do you know who lives
there?"

"No. That's precisely what makes my advice disinter-
ested."

"It is only with the greatest reserve that the Regent himself will speak of . . . You don't know who . . ."

". . . You're talking about. No, I don't—for the second time."

"You don't . . ."

". . . Know. No!"

Having said which I just had time to catch him and lay him back on the couch—and thank goodness I had offered him the couch. This was the real thing—tears, sobs, the lot. All right, I thought, let him get it off his chest; afterwards he'll go to sleep. Had I been a poet I would immediately have asked myself the cause of these tears, and in my turn decanted, by way of lachrymatory secretion, cascades of limpid, flowing alexandrines.

At last he calmed down, became coherent, reasonable . . . in fact it was in a rather too "good-little-boy" voice that he said, "I'm sorry. It's the awful news I received today. I just can't swallow the fact that father should want to get married again!"

This I found pretty hard to swallow myself! This night of confidences, the gathering storm, the somber beauty of the surroundings in which this young man had finally owned up to what he was . . . and I had glimpsed what he would become . . . The plans, the emotional collapse—all culminating in this dramatic reference to the paternal remarriage! I could only conclude that his tears must have overtaxed his resources. As for the problem of the still anonymous person who represented such a danger to the Regent—I gave up puzzling over it, since Leys himself, whose business it was, lumped it with the posthumous bigamies of a Belgian grocer!

But I should very much like to know which of the two things—my somewhat drastic advice to set fire to a corner of the Palace, or the letter he had received—triggered off the convulsion. He appeared to be genuinely panic-stricken at what I said. Well, we shall see. For today, or rather tonight, he is sound asleep.

He fell asleep on the couch, and I had my servants carry him off very gently to bed.

I stayed up, communing with myself, waiting for these clouds, alive with electricity and heavy with rain, to burst and shed their tears—easing with their mighty weeping the entirely intellectual anguish that has gathered and grown about this core: him—what he says—what he seems to be—what he is . . . ?

I have waited a long time. The swollen clouds have not burst. Not a flash of lightning in the sky. And in me, no release . . .

18 JUNE 1911

The invitation is well timed: now it is my turn to enter the Palace . . . by day, admittedly, and in the most official manner . . . The Envoy Extraordinary and Minister Plenipotentiary of France in Pei-king intends to present his credentials to the Regent, and the Legation has decided most opportunely that one more Frenchman in the procession will be all to the good.

I shall process, then—respectfully, yet keeping my eyes peeled for every detail once we are through the gate. I do not know where the audience is to take place—will it be in the Hall of Supreme Harmony in the middle of that high, white terrace like a vast, square plain, in that Palace we know so well from the enthusiastic and naïve descriptions of Europeans long ago, beneath the double roofs that form the façade and centerpiece of the noble complex of the Palace as seen from the top of Chien Men? I doubt it. The Ruling House is in mourning. The audience will . . . really, I have no idea where it will be granted . . .

Later I was the first of the "attendants" at the rendezvous— Tung Hwa Men, the gate I knew so well from outside. Inauspicious was the fact that it was a side gate, chosen no doubt to prevent us from seeing the way in by the Great Imperial Road that, having crossed the whole of China, passes through the

Chinese City, the Tatar City, and—last of its monumental verte-
brae—Ta Tsing Men, the gate by which it enters the Palace.
Never mind, I thought, I'll go in by the Side Gate.

The others began to arrive. Word went round that "the
Minister of France would be borne in a palanquin as far as the
audience room and that the party would . . . follow." (I am giving you a shortened version.) "Once in the audience room, as
soon as the Regent made his appearance the party would bow.
The audience over, the party would again bow three times and
withdraw backwards."

So this is what has become of the thrice three prostrations of olden times, I reflected. And I wondered how much diplomatic sweat had been expended over the reverences provided
for in today's ceremonial. As suzerain of all Asia, China used to
demand that her vassals and European "tributaries" alike submit to the great "humiliation"—forehead touching the ground,
body prostrate on the floor, and the whole performance to be
repeated nine times! The heads of embassies hesitated, and depending on their country of origin acted in very different ways.
The easygoing Portuguese obligingly agreed, prostrated themselves, and went away empty-handed. The more thoughtful
Dutch, with an eye to certain commercial apanages, also prostrated themselves, and met with no more success than the Portuguese. The Russians, out of good-neighborliness, did likewise,
much as they kiss one another on the mouth at religious festi-
vals in their own country, because this was the proper thing to
do. The English, before thus humbling themselves, required that
a high-ranking mandarin do the same before a portrait of their
King. (The high-ranking mandarin refused.) Only the French
ventured upon no such "humiliating" approaches. The fact is,
they never sent an accredited ambassador here. Their historical
memory and their honor are intact, I thought, as I strode through
the gate with head held high.

Inside, I tried to log my progress exactly. It was hard to
unravel that confusing network of gateways and rectangular,
symmetrical internal courtyards. I knew that running from

south to north was the axis and *raison d'être* of this reticulated Palace—the straight way, the median way . . . I determined to try and note the exact moment at which I crossed it . . . From time to time, pale-faced valets in blue robes appeared, stood still, and followed our progress with their eyes . . . They all belonged to one or another enclosure of those identical, vermilion walls, lived beneath roofs of the same yellow curvature . . . How, I wondered, should I ever find my bearings again? Must I, in this place where Diplomacy had brought me, ask my way?

How should I ever retrace my route on a map—how, above all, identify this place we were now entering . . . ? It was a kind of cave, civilized yet mysterious, drawing one in like the barely open jaws of the Imperial Dragon—a low-slung Chinese palace, all somber blues and greens inside, the only furniture a low platform . . . And it would have been empty, disconcertingly empty, had not the red-lacquered walls and wooden columns and above all the massive, inlaid, minutely carved and coffered ceiling furnished that emptiness and that absence with the richness of a royal treasure awaiting its sovereign lord . . .

I was still staring up at the ceiling with head thrown indecently back when someone gave me a nudge that sent me sprawling to the floor. It was high time. There he was, not two paces from me, alone on his little low platform, with us a couple of feet below him. The first three obeisances completed, I was able to look up and examine him . . .

But first, surprised by the suddenness of his appearance, I looked to see where he had made his entrance. Yes . . . there in the shadows of the northern wall was a low doorway, closed with a blue hanging that had just fallen soundlessly . . .

Young, fat, very gentle looking. Very "inoffensive" to be the object of such attacks, I thought. I could stare to my heart's content while the obligatory remarks were exchanged between our Minister, an interpreter, and him—compliments, wishes of good health, kindest remembrances to our President of the Republic . . . He wore the lesser ceremonial costume, in fact the mourning costume. It is not yet three official years since his brother, Emperor of the Kuang Hsu Period, was called away by supreme command to reign in the Heaven of the Sages . . .

So this was the man they were after! So gentle in appearance, with his round face beneath the conical hat—since the Manchu conquest the "Chinese" hat, official summer headdress, even for ceremonial purposes!—and his. hands invisible in the long sleeves.

His voice was quiet and serious—swollen, I thought, with an importance that is by no means entirely his own . . .

He finished what he had to say. The others made their obeisance. I made mine and, in obedience to protocol, still with lowered heads, we prepared to withdraw backwards. Poorly acquainted with the construction of Chinese buildings, the "party" stumbled over the great beam that lay solidly across the threshold.

When, breathing heavily, we picked ourselves up and ventured a last look into the depths of the cave, he was gone—swallowed up by the same theatrical device as had produced him. The blue hanging had been let down without a sound.

On the way out it was a different kind of letdown that engrossed my attention . . .

"All right in summer," an artillery lieutenant offered, "but think of the stoves they must need to keep all these shacks warm in winter!"

"Yes, and how about that," put in another of our number, indicating the White Tower, the Indian stupa that is so out of place in the Palace, "that tower thing like a 'Pippermint' bottle! Typically Chinese! Looks solid, doesn't it? Well, it's hollow inside—contains a tallow Buddha of an unknown religion!"

I can swear to the authenticity of these words. They were uttered in this instance by a captain of engineers. The word "tallow" no doubt did duty for "jade." And the bit about the "Buddha of an unknown religion" is pure nacre; it is the pearl of my treasury of Chinese inanities.

Only the Minister of France performed with spirit the re-

quired obeisances, climbed with considerable elegance back
into his palanquin and went off without saying a word.

Such, then, has been my first visit in person to the Palace.
I am dying to discuss it with him, and in fact he is supposed to
be coming at three this afternoon to take me to the theatre. I
have just had time to sketch hurriedly these first impressions
. . . Oh, how I wish I could recognize the way we went! I have a
large-scale (1:100) plan of the Forbidden City unfolded in front
of me—a European plan, to all appearances complete and exact,
in color, and bristling with transcribed names, but in fact a hasty
and somewhat childish piece of work drawn up by the Allied
troops during their occupation of the Palace in "nineteen hundred" . . .

And here, before my eyes, between my two hands spread
at less than a man's full span, I see, unfurl, spread out, hold, and
possess, at small financial cost, the plane representation of the
city as a whole, this capital and all it contains—Pei-king.

The shape of it, though unseen, is unforgettable once one
has lived within its confines—a Square set on top of a Rectangle. The latter—which forms the base, nothing more—is de-
formed and incomplete; its right-hand or eastern wall follows a
crooked, hesitant course. This is the Chinese City, seat of the
camp followers who encircle, snatch, and devour like ants . . .
This whole broad, southern part of the city could be swept away
were it not for the fact that it contains—fittingly for a *suburb*—
the two Temples, that of Heaven and that of Agriculture, lying
along its southern wall to right and left of the great vertebral
road.

This suburb communicates with the Square, the Tatar
City, by three gates.

The western one I never have occasion to use. The eastern one, however, Ha Ta Men, is my exit into the countryside
around . . . I know it only too well: it is *my* gate, my way of
escape.

The other gate, the one in the middle, is Chien Men. That
is all. There are no more.

Pitched solidly to the north of the Chinese City, then, is this Tatar City where I live myself, as a conqueror, but a most discreet one, down in the bottom right-hand corner. Square, or almost (it took European surveyors to show that its four sides differ in length), it raises walls thirty feet high against the plain around . . . This is my domain. Here is my property, for I possess a tiny square between the classical Observatory whose bronzes were cast by Jesuits of my race and the K'iao Leu, the corner pavilion from which this stronghold dominates the countryside, looking far out over land as flat as a calm sea, the alluvial sea of the plain . . . Then, enclosed within the Tatar City, there is the Imperial City, which by virtue of a poor play on words (untranslatable from the Chinese) based on the character "Huang" is often called the "Yellow City." Around it there is a further wall, though toward the east it is in a somewhat battered condition. And finally the third rectangle here, which the map makers were able to color a fine purple—by pure convention, all its roofs being in fact of the most beautiful yellow—the Palace.

I encircle it, dominate it, square my eye to its form: I comprehend it. The buildings, the courtyards, the open spaces, the different palaces of the Palace are all there, laid out with schematic symmetry like the cells of a honeycomb—rectangular, in this case, rather than pentagonal, but the feeling is the same: the whole hive has worked the wax for one of its inhabitants and one alone—the Female, the Queen. Four hundred million men gathered hereabout, differing no more among themselves than the workers of the hive, agglomerated these chessboard squares, these straight, sharp forms, these cells whose geometrical image—saving the angular depth of their roofs—is none other than the rectangular "parallelipiped"! But: sheltered, protected, defended against barbarian irruptions . . . in honor of the sole male inhabitant of these Palaces—Himself, the Emperor. And all this—metempsychosis or parable—projected onto the paper of my map without other reference mark or guide line than this great south-north axis which, after penetrating the Palace and its gates, abuts logically and precisely against the "Chung Kao," the Middle Palace, which on this plan before me bars the way . . . Just this simple indication of the center . . . But in practice—no idea how to begin to find my way about. Where is the path we followed today? Where did the Regent receive us?

Later the same day He arrived just in time—so I thought—to get me out of my difficulties.

"Tell me, Leys, which way did we go to the audience this morning?"

"I wasn't there," he said, smiling.

"Yes, I know, but I thought I might, with your help, be able to get my bearings a bit. Here, have a look at the map. I know I went in by Tung Hwa Men. Afterwards I crossed a bridge over a canal—possibly this one here, d'you see . . . ?"

But he hardly gave my map even a scornful glance, for all its paper precision. It clearly found no favor, spread out like that in the broad light of day, with one who enters there by night and knows his way about like a familiar.

I also had the feeling that his mind was on something else. Something was preoccupying him, I was sure of it. I folded up my map and let him take me off . . .

Had he perhaps found the means, I wondered . . .

At the theatre we were able to chat freely again, feeling as secure as on the most splendid evening in my courtyard. The sheer numbers of men sitting packed together on the floor around us, the garlands of thousands of women's eyes set in white, pink, and red faces looking down from the galleries, the music backed by the rich thunder of the gong—all this formed a delicate membrane around us, an atmosphere of which the very excess of color, smell, and noise fostered introspection. I was aware of how alone he and I were in this place. For one thing there were very few people who knew what we knew . . . His role, the mystery, the secret of the police . . . All his "friends," for example, who were sitting at a square table not far from us and who had greeted us so vociferously as we came in—wealthy, loose-living young men, that was all they were; they had no idea of the drama being enacted in the depths of the Palace on a stage very much greater than the one we had before us today . . .

René Leys, however, indicating the Big Bespectacled Fellow, said, "There's my secretary at the Central Bureau of the S.P. He's one of my best agents. He's amazingly strong under all that fat, and very sharp . . ."

"What—you mean even friends of yours . . . ?"

That "even," I thought, had been a little out of place.

But he replied quite straightforwardly, "All my friends are in it, only they occupy very different ranks, and none of them knows the ranks of the others. Nor are any of them aware of my own true position . . ."

And so we continued our secret and very frank discussion of police affairs in broken phrases of furtive French amid that Chinese crowd, now packed even more closely together, and amid the comings and goings of the servants who were flooding the tables with tea, tossing in the general direction of a dozen outstretched hands hot towels which were caught and, having discharged their office of wiping off accumulated sweat, hurled back with an elegant gesture resembling a wing beat or the movement of a fan . . .

. . . All of which I found more amusing than the stage crowded with coolie stagehands, chairs, which were intended to represent mountains, hangings of the most gorgeous Chinese crimson, which were to be seats of justice or red altars of matrimony . . . The tremendous din of the gong and the acid or azure whine of the two-stringed violin mercifully wrapped the whole scene in spangles of sound and a sustained, shimmering roar. But the character who had been standing there for half an hour weeping into his white beard with generous applications of portamento to the cracked voice of an old man who must have known Confucius at primary school—he was beginning to get on my nerves . . .

"But don't you recognize him?" René Leys whispered. "It's Prince Lang's nephew!"

Impossible, I thought. Yet there were those eyebrows, that arch of the eyes . . . An excellent piece of makeup. Yes, it was he. But how come his uncle let him go on the stage, I wanted to know. I had thought that in China it was the lowest profession but one, and moreover a stepping stone to the lowest which was . . .

René Leys interrupted me with a blush.

"Oh no! For ordinary singers perhaps, but he has taken up the stage so that he can sing in the Palace where it is very much the fashionable thing for those Princes who want to enjoy life and get in there . . . Besides, in the meantime he's earning very good money. You can hear—he's playing the 'Aged Father,' doing the 'cracked voice.' That's the one directors pay most for because it has a shorter working life than . . ."

There was a disturbance in the crowd. Several people around me stood up. Someone was pushing . . . I stood up myself. René Leys was already some way off, elbowing his way forward, muttering rapidly, and passing wherever he wished. I lost sight of him in the general bustle and began searching frantically for him in the absurd belief that he was in some danger. But he came back, and I saw some policemen hurrying someone out through the wings . . . a member of the audience, dressed in elegant blue silks, ghastly pale, fainting with barely a protest in the arms that dragged him away.

René Leys apologized for having left me so abruptly.

"I had to, I'm afraid. My men were showing some reluctance to arrest him. It's done now." And carelessly he added, "Oh, it's nothing at all! A eunuch who's been accused of talking too much and whom we didn't want to arrest in the Palace. I was able to tip my men off here. No one is going to come asking for him!"

"Do you think people noticed your rather . . . brisk intervention?"

"Not at all, no. A European can do the most extraordinary things as far as they're concerned . . . Do you think a Chinese, in a public theatre, would stare at those women the way we're doing?"

We were indeed staring with quite Latin insistence up at a balcony lodge which was full of familiar faces impasted with white makeup and bright with cosmetics and bosoms clad stiffly in silks of soft gray and pale blue hues, of crude purples, and greens "the color of the sky after rain" . . . It was our belles of the other evening, the lovely policewomen, displaying their triumphal charms ten feet above the shaven foreheads milling about in the pit—and a very much more attractive sight than the stage offered, with the nephew still mewling away . . .

No—his voice had given out and he had gone . . . And all of a sudden the spectacle, which according to René Leys was the grand finale of this ancient drama that had been running for a week already, became quite bearable to watch—full of colors, form, bright lights, and grand, flowing gestures . . . though I had no idea what it was all about. I simply watched as a tall man, dressed entirely in red, his face a red mask, a sabre gripped in each hand, came on and prepared to wage fearful combat—against what, did not at first emerge . . .

The sabres clove the empty air in a duel of which only one combatant was visible; his two armed fists played a game of evading and attacking one another; the two blades crossed and parried . . . A clash of steel? No—a pirouette, a leap, three moulinets and, on a crash from the orchestra, he stood transfixed, flinging heavenward his red mask and his two arms whose blades had been slicing thousands of scales in the air . . . The air was thick with spirits that he had just raised, I imagined . . . or rather sensed . . . And I was right, for at that moment they became incarnate and began their belligerent procession . . . The Red Man . . .

"He coaches the Imperial actors," René Leys whispered in my ear. "He's in charge of the Palace theatre."

Splendid, I thought, my whole attention now on the stage. The Red Man was already at grips with one of the incarnations —a black warrior, decked out in yellow, his face atrociously made-up, his back bristling with war arrows and flags, his eyebrows raised and extending from his nose to his temples . . . The portly figure of the hero combined with the rhythmic, dancing comportment of someone who is invincible and terribly sure of himself.

The swordplay recommenced with feints and leaps but still no clash of metal. There was something dreadful about the silence of those blades amid the wild tumult of the strings and woodwinds and brass of the orchestra . . . Ah!—the black-and-yellow warrior was beaten, mortally wounded; bowing his head, he received the deathblow on the back of his neck . . . and shuffled off into the wings, his part completed . . .

Another took his place, wearing other colors but presenting no less handsome an appearance. He fought with even greater valor to a different accompaniment . . . but was inevitably beaten in his turn, received the deathblow, and left the stage.

And so it went on, six times, the Red Man with the whirling wrists making feints, ducking and weaving about, parrying one blow and landing another, and yet—was it real fatigue or just consummate acting in a part that would kill one of our own athletes?—appearing to weaken, and gradually, before the last of his enemies, giving ground . . .

It did not seem to matter what the characters were thinking, what was really happening . . . And yet, I thought, supposing there were some drama underlying these gestures—a plot moving towards its denouement! Supposing all this action were merely incidental to . . . what? I did not know. I determined to ask René Leys afterwards.

But just then Leys volunteered somewhat inopportunely,

"Did you notice the fourth assailant? Talk about feeble! *And* he was a bit late coming on his toes!"

He was seeing the thing as a connoisseur, I realized. As for me, I continued to stare with complete absorption at the stage . . .

. . . where the motley band of defeated giants had suddenly resolved itself into a single man with a face of silver, blazing with strips and slivers of silver, bloated of figure and stiffly metallic of gesture . . . Him too the Red Man took on and vanquished.

Finally the Spirit with the face of gold came on—a vast sun borne on a pair of shoulders, executing a dazzling dance . . .

He was not really vanquished; he blew up with a bang—a firework tossed at his feet—and left the stage as the others had done.

The drama appeared to have run its course. The Red Hero was victorious; bathed in sweat, gasping for breath, he stood there uttering shouts of triumph . . . Was it all over, then? Already?

"No," René Leys told me. "Wait. I hope he'll be a bit better defending himself against the monsters." And he added confidentially, "He forgot to parade for 'number five.' "

I recognized then in René Leys the perfect theatre *habitué*. The drama being enacted on the stage means nothing to them. Whether it be Shakespeare's human *Hamlet* or the other so delicately travestied to the music of Ambroise Thomas, the great god Brahma in Léo Delibes' *Lakmé* or the great family soup in Charpentier's *Louise,* that monologue of the Sovereign People—the perfect theatre *habitué* ignores such nuances in the details of the libretto and concentrates only on essentials, on the quality of the *prima donna,* or the *portamento* with which the wretched tenor muffs a difficult "attack" . . .

And yet, I thought, what degree of penetration into Chinese—or better, Pekingese—life must this lad have achieved to be alive, in the midst of this eye-popping spectacle to which he had brought me, only to such minutiae!

For my part I could not take my eyes off the stage, on which the promised monsters now began to appear. First came a huge Symmetrical Devil who could turn himself end over end at will, having two faces, though not in the manner of Janus. It was quite impossible to tell whether he was dancing on his hands or his feet or a combination of both! The Red Man, slightly taken aback at first, fought with redoubled pertinency.

Afterwards there came a sort of living mass that was gathered up into a ball with neither head nor arms and that fought and eventually took itself off by rolling on its ubiquitous stomach. This was followed by an elastic monster whose arms, torso, and legs extended to deliver blows and retracted to avoid them. Then came a monster with the scaly head of a tortoise, and another representing a sea shell, and then an inhuman wheel spinning on the spokes of arms and legs multiplied by its speed . . . And lastly came the Simple Giant who would no doubt crush everything in his path because he was twice as big as anyone else . . .

The Red Man sprang forward and with a tremendous downward blow split him in two from skull to crotch. And with my own eyes I saw the two enormous halves fall apart from a cut that was horrible in its soft and bloody whiteness—and hurl themselves, one from each side, upon the Red Man who, wielding his two swords in crossed hands, held the divided monster at bay . . . until it disappeared like the others . . .

A breather at last, I thought . . . I was wrong. The Red Man, now in sole possession of the stage with nothing left to cleave in twain, began looking about him, bearding the emptiness, a prey suddenly to the most awful fear . . .

He was exhausted. Sitting there on the floor, leaning forward over outspread legs, he looked about him and was afraid. If one had only known of what! He was terrified. There was no fight left in him . . . He tried to flee . . . but could not. He leapt up . . . fell back, sat down again, and suddenly began to tremble in an appalling series of vertical jolts . . .

"You'd never think he was fifty-two," said René Leys. "Well, that's it. But before we go I wanted to . . ."

"Wait . . ."

He was really unbearable today.

"I promised to show you the solution I've found for . . ."

"Wait, will you! You're unb . . ."

"Do you see over there—to the right, just by the stage, in the Patron of the Theatre's box . . ."

Much against my will I looked and saw a Manchu woman in full dress making the usual simpering gestures . . . Who's she, I thought—another Policewoman? Fine. Splendid.

And my eyes were drawn irresistibly back to my absorbed, obsessive staring . . . The Red Man, alone in the middle of the stage which he had himself voided of its monsters like the stomach of a cooked fish, was in the very throes of terror! Sitting there with legs outspread, he went on jerking up and down on his buttocks in a pantomime of frenzy impossible either to describe or to imitate . . . until he fell over, and was finally still.

This time I was ready. I wanted to go. I wanted to get outside, fast.

How marvelous the fresh air was!

It has been longer than usual—three whole days—since I saw him last. No doubt he appreciates that his lessons in Pekingese mean less to me than his lessons in Pekingese life, and that the latter cannot, without risk of overexertion, be a daily affair. Or else he is pursuing his complex game somewhere outside of my house and of myself. It makes me a little jealous. For one thing I like him. I find myself beginning to accept him with the affectionate nonchalance one feels toward a person who makes you wait for him from one day to the next. I should find him hard to paint, if I ever had to paint him, yet he has a beautiful way of moving, whether freely through the air, or on horseback, or galloping through one of his stories with less fact or gesticulation than finely sustained mastery of the action and his description of it. And there is no forgetting that level look out of dark eyes suddenly dilated.

I have set out the couch and my armchair in the courtyard, still warm from the day's hot sun, as if I were expecting him . . . for further confidences . . .

There is thunder in the sky all around me. Thunder in the upside-down arena . . . the thunder that for days and days has been unable to resolve itself into lightning but continues to manoeuvre its chariots of sound on a tight rein round the horizontal circus above me . . .

I wait. What can he be up to tonight? What was he up to last night? I find myself keeping watch on his movements with the indulgence of an elder who is prepared to make allowances, and which is so much more effective than a father's! Grocer Leys away on his honeymoon can advisedly place his trust in me. It's all right, sir, I'm keeping an eye on your son. At least I count his absences more jealously than you . . . and believe I understand him better and am fonder of him than you.

That must be it—I am fond of this nervous, determined lad. What he says is perfect both in anecdote and tone. What he does . . . is either none of my business . . . or is bound up with what I have decided to love most of all in this world—the people that live in the Palace, successors, for all their paleness, to him who ruled and died in the depths of the Within! In evoking them for me, rendering them exoteric, he forms part of my *plan* of the Palace . . . a train of thought that brings me right up against this echoing wall—I feel a friend toward this nervous, vivacious youth, this giver of life, this conjurer-up of shadows . . .

"He was my friend"—the tone of voice in which he said that of the mysterious Departed One . . . the lone, sole male, spent with official pleasures, lord over eunuchs and women . . .

And then when he told me of his resolve to defend the Regent, the brother of his friend, against every danger, to save his life . . .

Why should I not be "his friend," then? He is shy—with fifteen years' age difference and our European reserve . . . He does not dare. It is up to me to take the initiative.

When he comes back here—if he ever does come back here—I shall suggest, logically, that he become, if he would like to, "my friend." I know in advance that he will invest the word with all the virtues I charge it with myself . . .

I know that few people can ever have exchanged such confidences beneath so heavy a sky . . . Is it to Heaven I must look for the resolution of this? He has not come. The night is bereft. Drops splashing on my flagstones tell me that at last the skies are easing, and that it is raining. At last!

Naked beneath my Chinese garment of flimsy summer silk, I receive the cloudburst on my skin and, refreshed, go off —at last—to bed and tranquil sleep.

It was just about dinner time—which I have unconsciously been making a little later each day. René Leys had himself announced and came in muttering hurried apologies. All was forgiven, I told him. I understood. No doubt a fresh attempt on the Regent's life was brewing. What would it be this time, after the bomb— the knife? Or the . . .

But I was a long way off the mark. I had spoken in haste. He answered calmly, "I have been very busy with my students. We're just in the middle of exams. Sixty papers to correct in two days!"

Disappointed, I recognized that my Conscientious Professor was back. We ate without appetite in the sweltering dusk.

Was he going to finish by unloading his father's love affairs on me again, I wondered, calling me to witness his career as the little orphan *manqué* repudiating the thankless author of his days?

But he spared me that . . . Again we sat bathing in the warm silence of night, and his altered voice took on the iron timbre of a certain bell I know as he reopened that door he had already led me through once . . .

As if echoing my words he said, "After the bomb, the knife. You don't know how right you are. It happened two days ago . . . It's . . . been the real reason for my absence . . . I have sworn not to mention it . . ."

He waited to see what effect his words would have on me. I was waiting simply for what would follow.

". . . . except to trusted friends who would help me in case of need."

A friend . . . and a trusted one! I have already mentioned my decision to be a friend to him. As for trusting, I trust myself on principle (otherwise life would be impossible!). And as for helping him in case of need—why not?

My silence alone appeared to satisfy him, like a discreet admission of enlistment.

"Good—now I can tell you. 'They' have been cooking this one up for a long time. I only heard about it twenty hours before it was due to . . . Ah well, it's all over now!"

He heaved a sigh, paused for a moment, and then resumed, his voice sinking at times almost to a whisper. And what a minute and logical account it was! A real masterpiece of policemanship. The young virgin of Chien Men Wai continuing to withhold herself, by order, from the second son of Prince T'ai, our young lover in expectation of employment had begun to multiply his promises: ingots of pure silver, dead pearls, false coral, a metal dressing case imported from England—even a Franco-Pekingese carriage with four wheels and springs, complete with team, and signed by the well-known carriage builder. Nothing availed. Abruptly the suitor made up his mind: he offered his Pure and Lovely Paracubine the chance, in giving herself to him, of becoming not a concubine of the tenth class, nor of the fifth, nor of the second, nor even of the first . . . but a princess, and much better than a princess—to become . . .

"Empress!" I cried, and it was like a hurrah.

Then I caught myself: "But there is an Empress already! A rather colorless one, it is true—Long Yu."

Continuing his narrative, René Leys agreed that I was not far wrong. No doubt the idea had been to get rid of the Regent first. A man had been found for the job. And the Prince, hoping

to draw a night's advance on his profits, announced to his loved
one the day before yesterday that the Regent would be dead before entering the Palace for the Grand Council on the morning
of the twentieth day of the sixth moon.

"Yesterday morning, you mean?"

"Precisely."

Events then followed one another rapidly. Leys received
warning at the "Arc de Triomphe of the East" restaurant in the
form of a pink silk handkerchief and immediately alerted his
best men, not one of whom was able to find the least trace of
irregularity in the escort of the guard on duty for the day, nor
anything suspicious in the streets along which the procession
was to pass, nor the slightest sign of anything at all, even an
electrical wire, under the bridges . . .

And yet just at the moment when the Regent, having left
his carriage, was about to pass on foot under the vault of Tsi
Ming Kung, someone had noticed, two paces behind him among
the gate guards . . .

"Who noticed?"

René Leys did not stop. *Someone* had noticed one character who did not bow quite in the way a well-trained officer
ought to bow. He was seized, searched, disarmed—for he had
been carrying a carving knife hidden up his sleeve—and slapped
into solitary confinement.

"And how did the Regent react?"

I always like hearing what people say when faced with
danger . . .

"The Regent saw nothing. He always keeps his eyes down
—it's the proper ceremonial posture. But of course he had to be
told . . ."

What must it have felt like, I wondered, to have been the
one who told him about it . . . about the danger? Or even more
the first person who suspected the man with the knife and
pounced on him? Who might it have been—the Captain of the
Escort? Would he accompany the Regent right into the Palace?

And I thought that if it had been him I would have given a lot to hear his story when he was good and drunk . . .

René Leys remained pensive a moment longer than usual. Was I doomed to remain in ignorance? At last he spoke—in that fine, confidential voice of his.

"Oh, it's no credit to me! I only needed to be warned in time. The man was easy to spot by the fact that the knife in his sleeve prevented him from bowing properly. I took him by the wrist in passing as if to tell him something and could feel he had a weapon there. As for informing the Regent . . . well, no one else was prepared to. I had no alternative . . ."

So it had been he. It really had been he. But I still wanted to know about the Regent . . .

"When he saw me turn up at what was not my usual time he guessed what it was . . . He went green. I told him, 'It's nothing. It doesn't matter. It's all over.' He realised that I had intervened and he shook me by the hand."

"What—the Regent thanked you just as Sadi Carnot would have done![7] Do you mean he knows how to shake hands?"

"By the thumb, I mean," René Leys corrected. "I did teach him once how to shake hands, but he always forgets the fingers."

Yes indeed, I thought. For I knew now what I had so much wanted to know. I had the Regent's hand in mine, or rather not in mine. I had the Regent's face before me . . . swollen with official, borrowed importance . . . I said to myself, What more need I know? I have truly, for the space of a moment, lived the most intimate life of the Palace.

And I marveled at René Leys. What a producer—no, what an *actor!* The part he had played bordered on the most courageous dedication . . . and not just in the moment when he had seized the man with the knife—what about the dangers beforehand, and the vengeance to come, now that the attack had failed? Like a conscientious judge I immediately wanted to get the facts of the matter straight. What had been done with the man with the knife, I wanted to know.

"In prison in the Palace. No one knows he is there."

"Who is he? An officer with a grudge? One of the Prince's men? A Prince himself . . . ?"

"No. A cook who had been reprimanded."

"No! How do you know? Has he confessed?"

"Not a word. He's paid to say nothing and he's saying nothing."

"What about torture? I mean, how do you know where he came from?"

"By his knife. I told you he had a carving knife which he was evidently in the habit of using."

Here we were down to the concrete evidence, I realized, the dazzling logic of the evidence. Nothing could oust this certainty: the attempt on the Regent's life denounced twenty hours in advance by the Lovely Policewoman and Virgin Mistress, and the promise of her lover-to-be, instigator of that attempt. The latter, second son of a Prince enjoying high favor at court, was a difficult man to bring an accusation against. Without a doubt he had acted in response to motives of a most lofty kind. What kind, though? What were his motives?

René Leys did not reply.

"Look here," I insisted, "I may seem to you to be indiscreet but it's because I'm thinking of the future. You have just saved the Regent's life. In doing so you will have gravely displeased the people who intended to deprive him of it. Aren't you afraid for yourself at all?"

My question appeared to plunge René Leys into a sudden agony . . . Had it never occurred to him before, I wondered incredulously. What a child he is. He really does need to have his thinking done for him. Someone has to keep an eye on him, and above all anticipate . . .

"Does the Regent's police cover you completely?"

"No, not if people can attack the Regent himself."

"Well, where do these attacks come from?"

"I've told you already—from the Within. But I've found a way of getting in there . . ."

"At last!"

"I showed you at the theatre—in the Manager's box to the right of the stage, that Manchu woman . . ."

"But the theatre was full of them!"

"That woman was a man—an actor!"

"So what?"

I was astonished that a high-ranking policeman should have been caught by such a thing. Ever since tourists, missionaries, and academics first started coming here the lowest journalist has been aware of the fact that, in the Chinese theatre, as in the theatres of some other lands, the female parts are very competently filled by males, the latter being subtler, slimmer, and altogether more elegant.

But he went on to explain: what was remarkable about this actor was that he is the first under the Manchu dynasty to be allowed to act in contemporary dress, namely in the costume of a Manchu woman.

"How did he get permission?" I asked.

René Leys did not answer immediately. Then he said, "By playing the same part in the Palace."

And that was the last word I could get out of him for the rest of the evening. It was almost as if he too were playing a part, and his part were over.

What an actor!

This time it is my turn to tell him my story . . . I would have said my "novel" had not the word become decidedly frayed as a result of thirty years of mistreatment and repeated violation on the part of the naturalist school. I refer to my interview, my wordless conversation, and—for lack of memories—my "hopes," the object of all three being the young Dame Wang.

For it was at her house, with her as my hostess, in defiance of custom and the Rites, that I spent yesterday evening. We were not alone, of course. There were sons, daughters, and sons-in-law present, issue of various beds but—fortunately for her youth—none of her own. They withdrew at a fairly early stage, well before the meal, which it would have been improper to consume en famille, as a mixed company of females and males.

It was thus to me, the foreigner, that they piously assigned the office of committing the impropriety. (And it is my earnest hope that, given time, I shall not fail to oblige.)

Three of us were left, then, sitting round three sides of the perfectly square, lacquered table—she, I, and her husband. I put him last not through any cheap and facile irony, certainly not (one can never be sure that one will not be a husband oneself some day); merely because it is the good man's own ambition to occupy that position. He hovered about us unobtrusively, talking in hushed tones, deeply honored to have me seated at his table, and openly flattered (or else I am very much mistaken) at the sedulity with which I was cultivating my neighbor, Dame Wang, and at the growing attentions with which Dame Wang rewarded my efforts.

To begin with, our intercourse was confined to the exchange of choice morsels of meat which passed to and fro at chopstick tip from one plate to the other . . .

Had I been a seeker after "impressions" or an editor in quest of copy I should infallibly have made a note of the quaint names that pinned down flavors and sauces of a classical bouquet remarkable for its elaboration, diversity, and sophistication . . . I had better things to do: the young mistress of the house, less officially daubed, more intimately adorned, could at last be appreciated in her specifically feminine aspects.

To begin with, her seasonal toilet (it is summer) was all slender lines; vertical yet supple; straight, yet rippling at the slightest movement, almost at the merest breath . . . A barely opaque material through which the air filtered, cooling the skin . . . A blouse with a round collar from which emerged a neck without perceptible anatomy, I mean with neither muscles nor leannesses, a round, moving, living column . . . Beneath the blouse, two modest breasts, precise of angle. And lastly a pair of legs that were incontrovertibly long. In fact I let my gaze linger on them the better to gauge their length . . .

After the meal the evening really began. An evening spent in the finest company of promises, adventures, ventures, and refusals . . . Granted, thanks to the tutor-husband our tête-à-tête was a prolonged one. Dame Wang was already aware that her person met with my unreserved approval, and the attention, the exaggerated politeness, albeit European, that I lavished upon her expressed better than my faltering and no doubt ridiculous words would have done my most fleeting shifts of emotion. I even reached the point—the rose or was it corn wine fostering brief illusions—of wondering whether the . . . natural conclusion might perhaps be possible (with the co-operation of night and the husband) . . . whether between the welcomed or tolerated foreigner I was conscious of being and this young Manchu woman . . . whether there might exist something—at the price of certain gestures, words, even money—beyond what was with us and would pass, namely an obscure state of desire or irony.

I looked at her. She was laughing at some gesture of mine. I amused her. I entertained her. But it amused me in my turn to wonder whether she considered physical love and all that goes with it as a childish game too (and it is a hypothesis) or as a shameful necessity, a service, a function, an adventure, a fashion, a moment, a habit, a well-drilled mannerism, a ceremony, a sacrifice, or as a ritual governed by chapter and verse of the physiological Bible instilled with the maternal milk in every fecundable female on earth and in hell!

Ah, if I were a novelist what short work I'd make of all this! A snappy three-hundred pager for three francs fifty!

Same evening   Yet I should dearly like to have even a provisional answer to this problem: can a normal, nubile European—to be precise, a Frenchman—aspire to complete possession of a young Manchu woman—likewise nubile, since she is officially married—and grace that possession with the name of "love" (without prejudice to eventual misapplications of the word)?

"René, my friend, tell me what you think—can a normal, nubile European love a Chinese woman, or more exactly a Manchu woman? And above all, can he be 'loved' by her?"

In these familiar terms I addressed the silent confidant of my long narrative. My confidant appeared to have taken in nothing. He stretched himself, yawned—yawned with both mouth and eyes at once, closed them, screwed them tightly shut, then flung them open as if emerging from another dream than my own and replied with careless boredom:

"No idea."

Then all of a sudden his voice changed. He stretched himself again, sat up, looked at me with that look I have come to recognize, and said slowly, reflectively, "Thank you, my friend, for calling me your 'friend.' "

Of course, I thought. It had been for me to take the initiative and I had done so. But this surely was worth a further confidence? And indeed, as if he had suddenly found relief, he poured it out:

"Do you know what the Regent offered me the day after that business of the knife?"

"Tell me."

"A concubine."

"Had he chosen well?"

"I haven't seen her. I didn't accept. I told the Regent I could never receive her at home . . . because . . . it's against European custom . . ." He blushed.

"On the contrary," I insisted, "it's a time-honored European custom!"

"I also told him that father would be shocked at the idea. And that furthermore my salary is not such as would allow me to support her in suitable luxury."

René Leys was genuinely and exceedingly embarrassed by this "favor." Yet it appeared the Regent had arranged everything in advance: the proferred concubine would continue for the time being to live in the Regent's palace where she would have her own private internal courtyard in which to hold court.

In my capacity of "friend" I felt the moment had come to offer my services. Strictly pecuniary, that is.

"Look, if you could do with a little advance . . . ?"

"Thank you," my friend somewhat coldly replied. "That same evening I was informed my salary had been doubled."

"Your professional salary? Two and two make four. Four hundred dollars a month. A thousand francs at the current rate of exchange. Not bad. My compliments."

René Leys was scornful.

"Two thousand taels. I'm talking about my salary as chief of the S.P."

"Ah! In that case my redoubled compliments!"

In fact, the sum was six times my very modest original estimate.

But none of this helped my problem. Could a Manchu woman be loved by a European, *i.e.* myself—yes or no? And could she in her turn lavish upon that European the usual attentions that are traditionally known by the name of "love" (in the poverty of our reputedly rich language)?

I despair of ever knowing. For at that point René Leys changed both key and time signature and began to talk in urgent terms of his father, his father's plans, and (horror of horrors!) his father's loves, if this ultimate prostitution be possible . . . his father's misplaced loves!

I was left with only one form of defense: to fall asleep, or rather to feign having done so.

15 AUGUST 1911

After that I recall . . . (I am slipping despite myself into the style that would be in order should I ever come to write this book . . . this book that will never be, for is it not better to live it? Problem.). After that came a number of days which recent revelations made flat and dull . . . René Leys has become regular again in his official tuition, matutine in his rising (he is always up before dawn), faithful to his mount (he always takes out the same animal, the chestnut that has thrown him eight or ten times in the street) . . . and comes back to me, his horse knocked up, at seven on the same morning as I saw him leave, the very moment at which I am struggling for wakefulness. He takes a shower, changes, and is off again, this time in a Chinese carriage drawn by an extremely fine-looking mule. Off to . . . ah, his College, of course. Time for his political economy class . . .

"No, I'm on vacation at the moment," he replied to my question the day before yesterday.

It's true. The University has been closed for more than two weeks. The end-of-year examinations are over. Where does he go, then? And above all, where does he find these friends who, variable as the phases of the moon, come along in ones, twos, and threes—never more than four—and expect lunch at such short notice?

They would be charming and also fruitful, had I the slightest hope of one day being able to speak something of their language . . . But the contortions involved would, I am convinced, tear the very tongue out of my mouth. They emit a mechanical eructation in which I recognize no trace of the accents of Northern Mandarin . . .

"It's because we're speaking Shanghaian," René Leys was good enough to explain to me once. He seems to be as much at his ease in this new verbal aquarium as one of those fishes with bulging eyes and a quadruple tail would be among the domesticated plants of my porcelain basin!

But really he and his friends behave so naturally and clearly feel so much at home here that it would be ill will on my part not to share in their well-being. After the meal their conversation becomes completely unintelligible to me. From time to time René Leys sums up for my benefit, in a couple of sentences of French, the gist of what has—perhaps—been said.

My guests leave "after the storm" that, in this season of the "great heats," breaks without fail between one and two in the afternoon. René Leys does not appear again for the rest of the day, nor indeed for most of the night, not until an hour that no paternal vigilance controls but that—to judge from my servants' knowing looks—encroaches excessively upon the morrow . . .

. . . The other fellow, though—Jarignoux—has suddenly become all too assiduous: two visits in a month!

The latter of these looked unpleasantly like turning into a kind of parental inquisition. No doubt he had had word from the father again, the remarried widower still uneasy about his son! And it was in order to be in a position to render account—or more exactly: "accounts"—to him that Mr. Jarignoux wished to know how the son was spending his time during the vacation.

When I replied that I had no idea, my inquisitor insinuated something to the effect that the Professors of the College of Nobles continue to receive their salary during the vacation, and that "one" wondered what "he" could be doing with the money.

I decided to ignore him. Perhaps Jarignoux would get the point and go.

But he was persistent: "Look, if I bring up this subject with you, it is on his father's behalf and in his own interests. And in yours too!"

"...?"

"He is seen coming in and out of your place all the time. Do you know ...?"

He dared not go on ... He would have been glad to have me interrupt him. I said nothing.

"Would you think the young man a libertine? Well, let me tell you, sir, he has no regular woman so far as anyone knows."

Not everybody is polygamous, I felt like telling him. He's a steady, orderly young man—that's all there is to it. But I said nothing. I was waiting for him to go ...

"You realize, sir, that it's scandalous your receiving him?"

"The French Legation receives him," I replied straightforwardly. "And receives you too, Mr. Jarignoux."

He was immediately up in arms. "The Minister is paid to. Besides, I give information: the last disturbances in Szechwan were reported by me."

I became gloomily meditative. Professionally or ironically, I reflected, the Minister of France must invite to his republican table numbers of people he would rather have eat in the kitchen ... Jarignoux broke into my silence.

"So all I have been telling you about him. as your neighbor and as a friend of his father ... leaves you indifferent—is that it? Well! Well ..."

I reflected again that out of politeness or discretion the Minister of France has to shake hands with all the Jarignoux' who have not as yet definitely compromised themselves ... I held out my hand. He went.

He went . . . And yet my neighbor's departure did not entirely dispel the odor of the eager insinuations he had thrust upon me. I had thus learned, much against my will, and it has stuck, that rumor gives René Leys no other female commerce than his visits to the singing girls of Chien Men Wai. I have sampled personally and can testify to the professional chastity of the latter . . . I have to admit, then, that all appearances are against him. And in his case there is not even the little Japanese girl on hand "for reasons of hygiene" . . . The young man is most maladroitly virtuous. Oh René, my dear René, you are either most unwise or else very poorly counseled in your youthful shyness . . . Must I, on top of everything, advise you like a mother on the eve of her daughter's wedding? No. Let him live down or else up to his reputation himself.

Even this calling him by his first name—a familiarity born of the freedom of soliloquy—I find irritating, and my irritation is quite naturally directed very much less against him than against Jarignoux. After all, surely René Leys has the best pretext one can have for *not* taking an interest in women in the plural—namely a woman in the singular. What need has he to go begging or hiring in Chien Men Wai when in the heart of the Regent's palace he has his own—by order?

I decided it was time to make discreet inquiries not only into the health of the young concubine but also . . . into the health of his amours with the same. I was diffident about putting my question, for on one or two previous occasions he had rebuffed indiscretions of this kind. Yet it struck me that simple morality left me with no choice!

"Tell me, old man—at what stage are proceedings with regard to . . . the Regent's little present?"

"Oh, not opened yet."

Marvelous! How aptly and concisely put! But I wanted to know why. Was the object in question not worthy the ungirding of loins? Must one assume untoward precedents? A whiff from the past? Might one, I asked, know the lady's official age, give or take a decade or two?

"Sixteen—Chinese reckoning," René Leys replied with precision.

That means fourteen or fifteen by ours.

"And is she pretty?"

René Leys thought about that for a moment, hesitating as if he had not really looked. Then he said, "You remember the sixth son of Duke Ch'ang who was sitting near us at the theatre . . . to our west, in the same row? I pointed him out to you."

I did not remember, but never mind.

"Perfectly. Fairly good-looking . . . young chap, long face, heavy eyebrows . . ."

"No—a round face with a small mouth . . . Well, my concubine looks exactly as if she could be his sister."

Why, I wondered, in order to depict his beloved-to-be, does he have recourse to the image of a chubby-faced youth?

"Tell me—I should love to know what attitude this living gift adopted at the offertory . . ."

"She tried to hide. She was very frightened. The Regent ordered her to stay beside me. She was very amused to hear me speak Northern Mandarin. She had taken me for a Manchu born in Canton of a Portuguese mother! I let her believe it. I couldn't have myself recognized, even with my European nose!"

"Why not?"

"What about the servants? And think of the S.P."

"That's true. Well, and what happened then—is that all?"

His answer took the form of a discreetly affirmative blush. René Leys said no more. Must he perhaps play toward her the same incorruptible role as Indubitable Purity performs in her Chien Men Wai fastness with regard to the Princely Second Son . . . ? Must he, perhaps, by a higher command, remain unswervingly faithful?

Faithful? But to whom? And if at someone's command . . . at whose?

I could tell by his face—that matte, unforthcoming look again—that now was not at all the time to voice this double doubt aloud . . .

Shall I ever know?

But then . . . does he, in his ingenuousness, know himself?

How the light is beginning to dawn! How things are beginning to fall into place! Words which at first hearing seemed ill-chosen now take on the precision of a . . . piece of arithmetic . . . a banking or police operation . . . Truly, I have nothing but admiration for this defender of the throne—of the altar, even (for the Temple of Heaven "changes hands" with each dynasty). He has managed it! He has penetrated to "the source of the danger"!

I admit he has had the most extraordinarily good fortune. Few Europeans, if any—no, not one, not even friend Jarignoux —can boast of having been thus "employed" to the full extent of his abilities by this government that remains lucid in spite of its age!

"But my dear fellow," I was unable to prevent myself from exclaiming, "my dear fellow, it seems to me that your position in this country . . . that you have a job . . . that the function you fulfill is, to my knowledge, entirely without historical precedent . . . At most you have a precursor . . . or two. There was old Marco Polo . . ."

"What do you mean 'old'—how old?" he interrupted anxiously.

Clearly he knew neither the name nor the age of this classic example of the Venetian comprador in China, the son and nephew of merchants, a merchant himself, and guest at the court of Kublai Khan, the grandson of the Khan of the Forts, of the Mongol Genghis Khan, Master of the Golden Horde ... knew not Marco Polo, citizen of Venice, who returned to his homeland, after seventeen years in the Khan's service, with his pouches bulging with riches and his mouth so full of adventures and tales of remote, foreign parts that people refused to believe him, indeed could not believe him ...

René Leys listened in some bewilderment, clearly flattered at being compared with this illustrious stranger.

Marco Polo (I pursued my monologue), son and nephew of Niccolo and Matteo Polo, who for more than ten years was Envoy Plenipotentiary of the Emperor of Further Asia, while back in Europe his homeland was at war with Genoa and Pisa and our good King Louis was crusading in Palestine ... On his return Marco Polo too wanted to fight for his homeland, and this Missus Dominicus, Envoy Extraordinary and Plenipotentiary of the Khan across vast distances of space, spent six months in a Genoese prison ... and thanks to this most timely detention had both the occasion and the leisure to leave us a book, the Great Bible of the Exotic, the Conquest of Elsewheres Beyond Belief, wondrous penetration of the realm of the Diverse, with the title—even finer than all it contains—*The Book of the Wonders of the World* ...

And René Leys had never heard of Marco Polo!

"Who was the other one?" he asked.

"The other one? Why—Sir Robert Hart."

There is a man every European must have heard of, I thought, that has set foot in this insipid China of today ... It even struck me that the compliment was a little overdone. I expected a modest denial from René Leys, a scrupulous examination of his merits as compared with the solid achievement of the minor English customs official who became Supreme Lord of the Imperial Customs and a figure in international finance. Yet in their beginnings there are certain similarities, and in

René Leys' case one must admit that ... promotion has been more rapid.

Evidently he agreed, for he professed to a very low opinion of Sir Robert.

"Father used to think he was a bit weak, a bit too taken up with the Chinese ... And he spoke Pekingese like a Shanghai comprador!"

It was then I felt I must set René Leys on "the way of confession."

"You were telling me you had found a means of gaining access to the Within?"

"What means was that?"

"The ... the actor who had so exceptionally received permission to dress as a Manchu woman ... Come now—the sole reason for your taking me to the theatre was to point him out to me!"

René Leys looked puzzled.

"But you must remember—on the left in the Manager's box ..."

"No, I don't remember," he said. "I can't have pointed out to you an actor dressed in Manchu costume—it's strictly forbidden."

"Oh, for goodness' sake! I have the most ruthless and indiscreet memory. I'm positive I registered all that."

Had I been honest I should have said "wrote all that down." And there I was, beginning to think I had made it up myself ...

It has got to the point with René Leys where I can almost guess what the dear boy is going to tell me next ... I had the feeling just then ...

And indeed, in a suddenly changed voice, he said, "Do excuse me for not having been here the last few nights. I was at the Palace, with rather a lot on my hands ... I was ..." he plunged on, "I was summoned for an audience."

"An audience? At night? But the Regent doesn't sleep at

the Palace! You don't mean the little five-year-old Emperor?"
He did not answer.

"But I really don't see who apart from the Emperor . . ."

"There's the Empress," put in René Leys modestly.

Of course . . . And rather ungallant of me. I was forgetting
the present Empress . . . and yet it was I who had first mentioned
her to him, I who had spoken her name for the first time. Since
the death, in all her ferocious beauty, of the Terrible Dowager,
Tzu Hsi, who in the span of her reign killed one husband and
Emperor, one son of her body and Emperor, and one nephew
whom she had made Emperor, and who governed both harder
and longer than her Far Western counterpart, that other "Old
Lady," Queen Victoria, who was more or less her contemporary
—ever since her passing the words "Empress" and "Dowager"
have not (for me) clothed a living reality. Occasionally the local
gazettes have come out with some ritual gesture aped from the
past, some colorless edict bearing the washed-out seal of "Long
Yu" . . . It was true—I had "overlooked" the Empress!

"She's the Regent's cousin, isn't she?"

"More than that—she's his sister-in-law! The Regent is
the younger brother of the late Emperor and she was his first
wife . . ."

This too was true, and this too I had forgotten. But in this
case the cousinship struck me as more serious, and of middling
political importance: the Regent and she are nephew and niece at
no very distant remove to the former Dowager, and both bear,
like their ancestor, the same Clan Name, a name of somewhat
evil augury since there is a prophecy, which is often on Pei-
king's more discontented lips, to the effect that the dynasty will
come to grief "through the fault of the Ye-ho-na-la Clan."

"My dear Leys—do you mean you know nothing of this
'ill omen' attaching to your friends' family?"

To which my dear Leys replied with confident assurance,
"The Ch'ing are more solid than they have ever been, and the
Regent is a much cleverer man than he gives the impression of
being. He accepts all the reforms . . ."

"Precisely. That's what I'm afraid of . . . and the assassination attempts . . ."

This brought me back to my questioning.

"You were saying, though, that the most recent attempt stemmed from the very part of the Palace you were anxious to penetrate . . . and in which it seems you have just been received . . . Tell me—isn't there a possibility that, if you'd traced the thing back from accomplice to accomplice, you'd have arrived at the 'Person' who summoned you to this audience? In which case—well done, my friend. No, don't say anything! You have most pertinently reminded me of the somewhat colorless existence of Empress Long Yu. I submit to you that her mandate is doubly restricted: by her own inadequacy, by the young Emperor's future coming-of-age—but also by the person of the Regent. If our Dame Long Yu has any ambitions at all the person of the Regent—living, that is—may well seem to her inessential to the general good of the Empire and positively detrimental to her own particular good. *Ergo,* in continuing to live, the Regent is acting in bad taste. If I were a melodramatist I should have no hesitation in running off a hundred thousand copies to the effect that Empress Long Yu had 'herself whetted the assassin's knife.' "

René Leys was silently disapproving.

I must go further, I realized. Screwing the thread of deduction ever tighter, I proceeded to muster my arguments. I became specific. I pointed out that the second, and possibly even the first assassination attempt came from a corner of the Palace to which neither he, René Leys, nor even the finest sleuths of the S.P. had ever penetrated . . . and that the chief sleuth himself, the same René Leys, had on the other hand just been summoned there in audience! I concluded—merely suppressing the numerous intermediaries—I very properly concluded that the Dowager Empress Long Yu was the sole and culpable instigatrix of the assaults upon the Regent's quivering skin (per bomb and knife) . . . and that the second son of Prince T'ai played the role of a mere confederate—possibly with pay—or lover, rewarded likewise in specie rather than in kind. I went on to accuse Dame Long Yu of being in love with the Princely Son whom, following the Regent's disappearance, she purposed to raise swiftly to the rank of Emperor-Consort, bestowing upon the still virgin singing girl the title—for life—of Twenty-fifth Washer of the Wedding-night Linen and honoring her, upon her death, with the official consecration of a magnificent triumphal arch of the kind reserved for exemplary widows and out-and-out virgins, which will stand at some busy crossroads and admit between its straddled legs anyone and everyone who happens to use the thoroughfare!

Extremely proud of my detective abilities, I insisted upon René Leys' remarking the lucidity of my reasoning: "Eh? I may not be on your S.P. payroll (yet) but haven't I hit the nail on the head? Haven't I smelled it out? How about it—yes or no?"

The way René Leys looked just then, I could just hear him answering as he had answered me once before, with stinging emphasis: "That's my concern!" In which case I should have replied, "All right—but then why speak of it to me?"

But he said nothing. He leaned back in his chair with a thoroughly languid movement and looked at me. It was almost as if he were preparing some lover's confidence . . . He! Heavens, I thought, that would really drive home Jarignoux's malicious assumptions!

At length he spoke.

"Let me tell you about Kuang Hsu's first wedding night . . ."

"Why do you call him 'Kuang Hsu'?" I broke in. "Surely you know his name!"

"Why do you want me to use the name it is forbidden to . . ."

"You're right. I accept the pseudonym. Go on . . ."

"Kuang Hsu, at the time he was told he must marry the present Empress, had never yet seen a woman . . ."

"Never 'seen'?"

René blushed like a schoolboy, betraying the fact that

"see" fulfilled the same function in his narrative as that other, no less active verb "know" fulfills in the Bible of the Hebrews.

"I mean," he embroidered, "that he wasn't used . . . He asked one of his friends for advice . . ."

This seemed to me the natural thing to do.

". . . and his friend said to him, 'When all the ceremonies, which will last from eight to ten days, are over you will find yourself alone with the Empress . . .' "

René Leys blushed again . . .

"Alone . . . no, one is never alone in the Palace. There are the eunuchs who usher one in and the ladies-in-waiting bustling about . . . Anyway, that was what his friend said to him . . . 'Eventually you will be told that all is ready. You will go up to your wife, you will lie down on top of her, and you will act.' "

Once more René Leys broke off.

Yet it struck me that no advice could have taken a more classical form nor been more refined as to language nor more vigorous as to pertinency. I could find no fault with it.

"The Emperor, anxious to please his friend by following his advice, went up to the Empress and lay down on top of her. But then, having, during the eight to ten days' festivities, drunk rather too much wine, he forgot to act, and fell asleep . . ."

I gazed at René Leys in admiration. Nothing could have conjured up in a more anguished fashion the spectre of the departed Impotent, the Non-Consummator for Reasons of State . . .

Was he really aware, I wondered, of the value of his words? And above all, who could have told him all this? A eunuch? He would not have understood! A lady-in-waiting . . . would never have dared . . .

Should I ask him where it came from, I wondered—this so special, so conjugal story? No, I would never dare myself . . . In any case I saw he was lost again in a languid dream, his dark eyes wide beneath the dark sky . . . I felt it would be indecent to interrupt . . .

Suddenly he sat up.

"Do you know how much my first 'night' in the Palace cost me?"

Absolutely no idea! I had no criteria . . . And anyway, I wanted to know, who had to be paid?

For René Leys the answer was obvious: the eunuchs had to be paid.

I made a rapid calculation. Ten per cent is the figure Europeans will usually run to in their dealings with Chinese servants . . . but in this case the servants were all extremely high-ranking officials! And then—ten per cent of what? I threw out at random a figure which I thought pretty high . . .

"A hundred dollars!"

. . . and was treated to René Leys' perceptible scorn; for one thing I had couched my answer in terms of dollars, which represent barely seven-tenths of the true tael, the ounce of refined silver cast in those navicular ingots called "shoes" . . .

But how about you—do you know, in taels, how much René Leys had to pay?

"Three thousand four hundred—cash."

And that merely as a "by your leave" at the Gate, just to be let through. Moreover, the whole thing was handled with the strictness of a commercial transaction. He had an official receipt, he told me . . .

And he handed me a slip of paper covered with characters of such cursive abbreviation that they simply lay there in my hand, powerless to clarify in any way what he had just been saying . . . In the last light of my flickering lamp I stared at them, but they were as much of a mystery to me as a piece of Egyptian stenography swathed in Hittite arabesques, studded with cuneiforms and scraped for a living by twenty archaeologists!

I looked up in stupefaction and was about to return his slip of paper—a precious document, I reflected, this receipt against three thousand four hundred silver taels for a first night in the Palace—when I noticed that, this time, he was well and truly asleep.

I committed the precious paper to one of my pockets and put off till tomorrow the sequel and conclusion of this marvelous "first night" . . .

A fresh adventure! And a fresh blow to my perspicacity! How could I ever have compared René Leys with Sir Robert Hart or even with Marco Polo? How could I ever have coupled the name of this most admirable son of a Belgian grocer with those of a minor English customs official and the nephew of Venetian merchants? I should never have told him: You are on a par with Sir Robert Hart and *Il Milione!* I beg him to forgive me, for what I ought to have said is: You have gone further in your penetration of China than any other European known or unknown . . . You have attained the heart of the center of the Within—nay, better than the heart: the bed!

For lo and behold, this novel of intrigue and detection—if I should ever be seized with the indecent idea of actually writing it—has all of a sudden owned up to its hero, a real, live, genuine hero, in the person of the rarest bird of all the trashy novels of the two worlds—the Phoenix! The hero is in fact a heroine. The Phoenix is female. There—I have already said too much: every Chinese reader of these notes will have understood. Yet, having understood, I doubt if he will do as I did and *believe.* It takes the receptive credence of a traveler from abroad who is in love with this country to accept without a qualm what a native reader would brand as sacrilegious, immoral, shameful, incorrect, unwonted . . . And yet how logical, necessary, inevitable is everything that follows! Words that might initially have seemed clumsy become precise in their meaning—and I pay the full tribute of admiration that is due, richly due, to this triumphant lover, this conquering René Leys! What a requital for the attack on the Legations in 1900! He has laid siege to and vanquished the heart that is imperially sealed, the Triple Person quadruply enclosed, the Inexpugnable, Mother of the Empire, Ancestress of the Ten Thousand Ages!

It is in fact this last point—differences in social position and race being eclipsed by a mere age difference, particularly as regards the older party—that prompts me to believe in this miracle of love. Counting "historically" I find that Dame Long Yu has between thirty-eight and forty years of her own. He is not even eighteen. The chronological probabilities are high!

And furthermore I have the documentary proof. It is as if at each fresh adventure, each fresh revelation, René Leys is at pains courteously to provide me with my reasons for believing him. Three days ago it was the official receipt for that "First Night" . . . (I must bring myself to give that back to him—he will probably need it to negotiate the second.) Today it is a prose poem, a kind of lyric epistle. (The paper, incidentally, is perfectly ludicrous—flowers of an artificial blue against a background of green and sentimental pink, with a moiré envelope in cream and a flaccid beige.)

It begins: "My dear Victor . . ."—so sudden?—"I take the liberty, on the strength of our previous talks, of addressing you in the familiar form in prose à la Chinese as good friends do in verse. I am writing to tell you that you spoke to the point when you asked me: Can a Manchu woman love a European, and be loved by him in return? Allow me to tell you that it is possible and that I know from personal experience. Since you are interested in everything that concerns Her"—the Imperial capital letter—"as I am myself, I hasten to communicate the following. Yesterday, finding the weather too warm, She had the idea of an outing *together* '—sic—' on the 'South Lake.' It was evening. The last rays of the Sun were gilding the tip of the White Tower and there was a light mist on the lake. I can still see myself, dressed as a mandarin of the fourth grade, sitting: beside her palanquin, behind which stood two eunuchs and three ladies-in-waiting, plunged in my thoughts to the gentle motion of the Imperial boat. Suddenly I heard a sound of gongs and drums behind us: some eunuchs were following in another boat, singing classical songs, which were quite unlike those I have learned at the theatre in Chien Men Wai but no less charming . . .

"When we had left the boat and were more to ourselves in the orange room, She showed me a poem that she had written while waiting for me, and that ran:

" 'Why can the loved one not be forever at Her side?

" 'Do not the fish and his mate swim together in the lake whose waters are dyed five colors by the leaves of the ten thousand trees that stand admiring themselves' "—sic—" 'on its shores . . . ?

" 'Do not the peacock and the peahen fly wing to wing through the balmy air?

" 'But I believe I see him—a familiar anguish throbs in the Phoenix' breast.' "

The rest of the letter is less poetic, reverting to prose for a kind of commentary:

"My dear friend, you can imagine my sadness upon finding myself next morning giving my class in political economy! My room is on the first floor of the Western Building and the yellow roofs of the Imperial Palaces are visible from my windows . . . I could not help thinking that beneath those roofs lived She with whom I had been talking the night before. . .

"What do you think? Does this look well among the 'documents' and souvenirs you are collecting about Himself?

"P.S.: Do not, whatever you do, neglect to tear up this letter!"

. . . Done.

3 SEPTEMBER 1911

I was wrong. I should have kept that letter—the first, or at best the second, I have ever received from him. Today's is the third. It would have been a fruitful exercise to compare them with the first little notes of apology he was sending me some months ago ... There the writing was awkward and childish ... It still lacks decision but it now makes liberal use of dashes and has adopted a certain slant. Several of his capitals have definitely taken on a new form, and one moreover that I recognize as familiar. The M with its two harshly vertical downstrokes, the W with its horizontal extension, that S, which can only be written from bottom to top ... I know whose handwriting he has borrowed those from—my own! Well, there's a surprise! Here am I, carefully noting the Chinese influence emanating from this master of Pekingese life, and never suspecting for a moment that I have been exerting a surreptitious calligraphic influence upon him. But the evidence is staring me in the face. Intrigued, I read it over again, in spite of its banality:

"My dear friend, I need some advice from you." Prosaically he has resumed the polite form of address. "Shall we go for that ride early tomorrow morning? We did talk about it, I believe ... Cordially yours, René Leys."

It is true. We agreed to go for a ride together one morning

—very early. But what is important here—the ride or the advice he needs from me? And advice about what? About his Chinese official life? I disclaim competence in advance: he seems to be doing well enough by himself. About his unofficial life? Would he be needing ... the kind of helpful hints that people infallibly thrust upon the newlywed? Or does he intend to become the vindictive son and want me to dictate him some "disrespectful remonstrances to his father?"

I shall know tomorrow ...

. . . And without even leaving me a decent hour in which to wake up, there he was! It was certainly a fine day but almost too early yet to tell whether it would remain that bright blue or turn a leaden gray. He predicted marvelous weather, inhaling the fresh, cold air deeply . . . He swept me off with him . . . and in no time we were out in the open countryside, riding through fields of millet whose stems overtopped us even in the saddle, along canals that in summer are full of warm water, across the vast plain that stretches from the sea to the mountains and holds, contains, upholds, surrounds, waters, and feeds my city, my Capital!

His mind was on none of this, however . . . Choosing his moment, he asked if we might slow our horses to a walk (none too soon for me, for we had set out at the pace of a two-mile steeplechase!) and repeated what he had said in his letter.

"I need some advice from you."

"All right."

"I should like to know what you would do in my place."

A necessary preliminary, I pointed out, was that he should put me in his place. What was it exactly?

"You remember that concubine—the one the Regent offered me? . . ."

"Yes."

"In my place, what would you do with her?"

Astonished that it had not yet been "done," I was about to suggest he follow the advice of the friend of his friend "Kuang Hsu"—"You will lie down on top of her and you will act." But he cut me short.

"I don't mean . . ." and he blushed. "The thing is, I don't know whether I should accept her officially."

"Oh yes, do accept her, believe me, do accept her, even if only . . . unofficially. You told me the young offering was not unpleasing either as to age or as to form. Or are there perhaps considerations of a . . . 'diplomatic' nature?"

He seized the proffered branch.

"Yes—'diplomatic': *She* would no longer allow it."

He gave the pronoun "She" the Imperial capital usually reserved for "Himself," doing so by means of an inflexion of the voice that is the equivalent of the respectful raising of the two joined fists . . .

Then he fell into one of those belated silences that almost invariably ensue when a person pretends, after the event, to have "said too much."

It was my turn to set off at a gallop, for I needed an outlet for my keen delight! I was ridiculously happy! He had just confirmed—and with what naked honesty!—the poetic confession made in his letter . . . The boy is marvelous, I thought. Alone it would have taken me ten years to open by one crack the little low door of which he had just thrown both leaves wide for me.

When I slowed down, somewhat out of breath, he was at my shoulder, repeating his question with an attentive air.

"What would you do in my place?"

"In your place I should first give myself a pat on the back for having come so far . . . Then I should try to stay there as long as possible. The audiences of great ladies are governed by a pretty capricious protocol . . . And I should confidently expect that, having been opened in my face, the door would be shut again behind my backside . . . "

I was sure this was the right way to answer him . . . He must not be allowed to mount this great horse called "Empress's Love." Above all, he must be prevented from taking the thing too seriously . . . I could see it all and was certain my advice would do him good. The Empress had condescended to cheat her widowhood by amusing herself—for a few nights—with this young European of "romantic" lineaments (and he really is handsome, even to Chinese eyes), excepting, that is, a nose that I consider perfect and that the same Chinese eyes must regard as a "hooter," but that She no doubt forgives him as being a sign of breeding (as one forgives the monkey with the prehensile tail his horrible hairy appendage).

With telling precision, however, he put everything back in its place. It was not a question of preparing for eventual disgrace (he seemed to be very sure of himself on this point). All became clear. The struggle was neither tragical, nor biblical, nor comical; even less was it fought with the passion so dear to the Hugolaters. No, it sprang entirely from the discipline he professed at the College of Nobles—Political Economy, under which head I include both public politics and private avarice—and was summed up in this admission to end all admissions:

"I can't afford to offend Her," he said, using the Imperial capital again. "My whole job depends on her!"

The fundamental question underlying everything was whether his monthly salary would be increased or stopped. That was all! The little bit of love that might by some extraordinary chance have stolen between the millenary mistress and her youthful lover . . . had failed so to steal! For the first time I felt disappointed in him.

When you think about it, though, and particularly when you come to add it up, his "job" does seem to be pretty worthwhile. Leys Sr. need have no qualms about his son's future—or present, for that matter. He told me at lunch today not only that he is entitled to wear the "Horse Jacket" but also that he has been appointed "Grand Treasurer and Paymaster of all the Princes of the Within"!

I did not know which to congratulate him on more. The right to wear the "Ma-kua" or "Horse Jacket" is without doubt a very great honor indeed. The "jacket" in question—though a real garment, yellow in color—is actually more in the nature of a hat, rather like the headgear worn by Spanish grandees and retained nobly on the head in certain churches where they enter on horseback. René Leys is proud of it because up to now this yellow garment has been worn only by a few Princes of the Blood, the Dukes of the Iron Helmet, and one or two former Chinese councilors . . . And Grand Guardian So-and-So and the Mongol Princes So-and-So and Such-and-Such and the Viceroy of the Two Hu and many others have never, never managed to get it.

That is the point, of course: the special quality of this "order" consists pre-eminently in the scorn in which those who possess it hold those who have missed it by a hair . . . Which makes this "distinction" not unlike all orders the world over . . .

The other title is a very much weightier and more resounding affair. René Leys began to calculate for my benefit the monthly allowances that, from now on, it is his job to pay out to each of the Princes. The worthy Pu Luen, for example, well known in European billiard-playing circles and yet ex-heir to the throne by virtue of his direct ancestor Tao Kuang, sixth Emperor—Pu Luen "draws" eleven thousand taels every moon. The Regent fifty-five thousand . . .

"As for the Dowager, Long Yu, apart from her privy purse, do you know how much her title is worth to her—'Long Yu'?"

"Yes, I know her name is Long Yu."

"That's not her name. That's a title given her by the Regent—a title that puts her above all Tung Chih's old concubines. It brings her in ten thousand taels—extra—a month."

I feigned bedazzlement. Did two words, two honorific characters, possess, in China, such vast financial power? I began to see how solid René Leys' "job" is.

"You strike me as being in an excellent position," I concluded. "At one and the same time you are friends with the Regent and . . . friends with the Empress. You reconcile the dynasty in your person . . . It is a great service you have done them . . . What recognition have you received?"

Modestly, precisely, he replied, "I have been informed that my salary has been increased by fourteen per cent . . ."

Oh no—I wasn't going to risk asking "fourteen per cent" of what! It must be something pretty extraordinary. I can confidently congratulate him!

And yet there is no doubt of it—he loves and is loved. It is not just his capital letters that are beginning to straighten up and adopt a virile stance. His whole bearing, which before was that of an adventurous child, has become transformed into a staid, self-satisfied contentment . . . tending to be slightly withdrawn on mornings after the big audience . . . Something definitely seems to have been developed, metamorphosed, revealed . . .

Could it be . . . ? And suddenly, as I reflected, this doubt assailed me—is the Empress perhaps not, for him, just another lover but . . . could it be possible . . . his first, his Initiatrix? There are a number of reasons for supposing so. It is an extremely delicate matter on which to press him . . . Awkward enough, despite the tokens, in the case of a girl, the question becomes virtually impossible to ask in the case of the sex to which I owe my own . . . But it occurred to me that of course Poetry, properly understood, permits of every licence, and what can never be expressed in vulgar prose it is still possible to put into rhyme . . . He himself, who couched his revelations of that "First Night" in the form of a poetic letter, gave me the idea of extending the correspondence in the same vein.

I thus composed the following poem, copying it out with great care onto a piece of paper decorated with pale, lacy flowers, transparent and highly indiscreet.

"On that nocturnal day when the female Phoenix received the son of the foreign Eagle in her nest,

"Which of the two trembled with love or with ignorance? The Phoenix, mistress of a long life already, knows everything —and much besides.

"But the son of the widowed Eagle has only just spread his wings: he beats them precipitately, and succumbs.

"Which of the two will bare for the other the bosom of happiness? Who but she, the eternal, maternal Phoenix herself,

"Who greets him, keeps him, receives him whose every step she anticipates and provokes!"

I should very much like to have written this poem, which I venture to dub "occasional," with a single stroke of the brush in the style of the ancient "Chou" bronzes. I had to content myself with translating it into French—from a nonexistent Chinese original.

Abstaining from any comment—it seems to me quite clear —I have dispatched it by post to Mr. René Leys, Professor at the College of Nobles. If he understands, he will reply. It is hardly insulting, after all: I have drawn upon poetic licence to the extent of turning a grocer's son into an eaglet!

He understood all right, but he did not reply, at least not in the medium of poetry. Far from sending me in return a poem which took up the same rhythms (as is customary) and as it were, echoed them, he merely said on this first evening on which we have recovered the intimacy of the early weeks of our friendship, sitting on my terrace before the night whose darkness challenges honesty, he merely said, with kind familiarity:

"It was well written, your little Chinese letter—almost like 'characters greeting one another.' I got the historical allusion . . . Yes, it was She who (. . .) me."

I omit the verb purely out of Chinese decency. Although it dates back to the most venerable antiquity, in modern French it is known primarily in an entirely converse usage, which draws upon the heroism and conquering connotations of Joan, Maid of Orleans![8]

So my suspicions, or rather my ratiocinations, were correct. In precise, police language, "The Virgin at length bestowed herself upon the Prince" (if we change round the sexes). Splendid. But which of the two ought I to congratulate? Her, for having chosen with such taste one not of her race? Him, for having been chosen by Her? Here he is, I reflected, Chief of the

Secret Police and unofficial lover to Her who is not even al-lowed any official ones! The Friend of the Regent! Titular of a young concubine offered him by the said Regent! Recipient of the "Horse Jacket"! In short, a young man who has most defi-nitely "arrived"—and that before reaching the age of manhood! Consequently . . . a happy young man?

Very gravely he shook his head.

"No. There are problems. I am worried about the South-ern Provinces." And in tones of the deepest confidence he added, "This Sun Yat-sen . . ."

On this point I was really able to reassure him.

"My dear fellow, you mustn't trouble yourself for a mo-ment about him. Sun Yat-sen! Why—when I mentioned him before, you didn't give him a thought! Come now—admit that I put this Cantonese flea in your ear. Dangerous? Let me show you . . ."

And with my right thumbnail I crushed an imaginary parasite sitting on my left thumbnail. I pretended to blow the remains away.

"Let the dynasty do the same and the insect and its revo-lutionary itch will vanish together . . . and there will again be long days of rule and long nights . . . of love. By the way, you have never spoken of your own except in terms so poetic that I have had to imagine the reality . . . in which, however, you are present only in spirit. What happens from the 'fleshly' point of view?"

I could detect no blush as he answered my challenge.

"There is the prescribed procedure . . ."

I told him I should very much like, if not to learn that pro-cedure—the broad lines of which I believe date back to the ear-liest antiquity—by heart, at least to pick up its finer nuances . . .

And with the best will in the world he proceeded to sat-isfy my curiosity. He even anticipated my first question.

"How do I get into the Palace? Dressed in the costume of a Manchu Princess . . ."

"Aha!"

". . . which I exchange, once I am inside the walls, for the costume of a mandarin of the fourth grade."

"Ah yes, that's better. I prefer to picture you as a man. Then?"

"Old Ma—you know, the titular eunuch who succeeded Li Tien-ying, the Aged Dowager's lover—Ma comes in person to take me through the other gates as far as the courtyard of the Eastern Palace, where I am greeted by the eunuchs on duty in the Apartments."

"How—'greeted'?"

"They always have a tactful word for me. Last time they said, 'Our Mistress awaits you most especially this evening.'"

"Oh, very delicate!"

"I pay them well. Do you know how much the last night cost me?"

"No . . ." I said, deciding not to venture on any more calculations of this kind.

"Five hundred taels!"

"Is that all? It seems to me very much less expensive than your 'First Night.' Is this one of those 'tapering' tariffs, then?"

"Yes. The first time I paid five thousand . . ."

"I beg your pardon—three thousand four hundred! I have a note of it. I remember to within a sapeke . . ."

I even have the receipt, I should have added, had it not been for the fact that, ever since he was good enough to give it to me, I have carried it around in my pocket, ashamed of my inability to decipher it . . . He seems to be able to do very well without it.

"I've come to terms with them since then. I get in for much less. I spent a *t'ung-t'ung* with a Prince who is very anxious to get into the Palace at night. We pay a lump sum."

I for my part was very anxious to get back to details of a rather more poetic nature.

"Tell me—in this 'audience,' what rights are you accorded?"

"Oh, I don't make any demands. That's not where one brings up one's serious proposals. That's at the Ministry of the Interior. For example I've just been appointed . . ."

I stopped him.

"I believe there is some confusion of ministries here. I expressed myself poorly. What I meant was—is the Empress as strict as the young policewoman of Chien Men Wai . . . do you see? Of course, it's none of my business whatever . . ."

But René the Triumphant clearly did not begrudge me the domestic details. A few words made me an eyewitness, as it were, of each of the prescribed acts. I discovered how they lie down on the warm bed, which is made of hollow bricks and upholstered with silk cushions and which in winter is heated like an oven through the aperture in the side by means of a fire of sweet-smelling herbs. Thanks to him I have really penetrated to the most private center of the Palace. He is young enough to tell as amusing stories between friends all the things that the mature conqueror of the fair sex keeps jealously to himself. He told me, for example, with perfect candor that "she is not as fat as her portraits make her look" and that even in a state of undress she retains that "little triangle of silk that hangs down between her breasts and her stomach, forming a kind of high belt in the Manchu fashion" . . . And the rest, all the rest, was mine in a few words.

So why weary myself with pointless caviling at this little triangle of silk . . . perhaps some hygienic device to protect against unbilical chills, possibly the little-known emblem of some Buddhist order having the power to cleanse every gesture and purify all the guilty pleasures of amorous dalliance . . . ?

"When winter comes," he went on, "the brick bed is officially heated. From there the heat spreads into all the other rooms and the woodwork begins to give off a lovely smell. They use sandalwood and cedar especially for this reason. The whole Palace begins to smell beautiful."

I saw. I smelt. I believed. I felt endued with perfume . . .

"But it's summer now. Who told you how beautiful it smells?"

"She did," was his simple reply.

For a moment he was lost in dream, and it struck me how well the posture suited him.

"Do you know what we talk about when we . . . lie beside one another?"

I smiled. It was my turn to be delicate.

"The Chinese term for it is 'pillow talk'!"

"No, no! We talk . . . about other things . . . about . . . anything."

"I envy you . . . And I congratulate you on the fact that you can be alone with her like that . . ."

"Alone? We're not alone at all!"

He was amazed at my congratulations, at my envy. Alone? And the eunuchs, whom there was no getting rid of? (Though how little they counted!) And the ladies-in-waiting? All the "zealous little servants" of whom the Book of Odes spoke three thousand years ago and who have not ceased since then to perform in every place and at every hour of the day and night the minutest services for the Princess whom they never leave any more than the satellites leave their mother planet . . .

I complimented him on remaining so perfectly literary and traditional. In his place I should have felt rather less at my ease.

And yet he has taken me further than I should ever have boasted of reaching! Thanks to him I know "everything—and much besides" (the quotation is already historical). Perhaps more than he himself, I reflected, as he suddenly became a child again, concluding:

"I was very scared when at four o'clock in the morning I found myself for the first time inside the Palace where it is for-bidden to admit any man—except the Regent and the members of the Grand Council—under pain of death."

"What kind of death? What would they do to you if they discovered?"

"Nothing!" He burst out laughing. "Nothing—I'm a European."

It's true. But really—tonight I needed him to remind me. It's true, of course, and it explains and excuses everything—he is a European!

By dint of a fresh effort I realize how much my life here in Peiking has both expanded and contracted ... For a start I have lost the lessons and visits of Master Wang ... Can he have taken offence at the attentions which I quite naturally lavished upon his wife? Or was it my interest in his co-tutor René Leys? Anyway, he has gone, as soundlessly and discreetly as he came, stating in his letter of apology that one of the Princes for whom he used to work at the Ministry of Rites has asked him to resume his services, those services being required at an hour which clashes with the time of my lesson.

It is a polite excuse. Utterly phony, in the Chinese manner, but polite. My tutor has elegantly given me the sack.

To make up for it, my other tutor has once more become punctual and matter-of-fact in the discharge of his duties. I am no longer nearly so surprised at the things he tells me. All his movements in the Chinese environment are characterized by the easy freedom of a carp that has lived ten years in the same basin and could feed, see, and move about even without the aid of his great big eyes and quadruple tail. There it is. This young man, though nubile and still virgin, this young man who is so gifted when it comes to acting and speaking in Chinese experi-

enced no more awkwardness at finding himself, for "diplomatic" or other reasons, with an Empress in his arms than he
did the other night at the restaurant when, as a dare or as a
practical joke, the sixth son of the Mongol Duke Ngo Ko thrust
into his hands the public violin that is to be found on all the
tables of every private house in Chien Men Wai . . . What did
he do? He played it—of course.

I feel much heartened, and very happy.

Later Why should it have been at that very moment that my
boy handed me that ridiculous letter—that utterly vile and dis-
graceful letter that just asked to be thrown in the wastepaper
basket without a reply! Not having a wastepaper basket in my
impeccably Chinese study I screwed it up into a ball and in my
rage threw it right across the courtyard and over the stable roof.

As I remember, it ran approximately as follows:

"Sir, since you are so interested in one Leys, René, and
are privileged to put him up nightly on your premises—perhaps
you would be interested to know that he owes me fifty dollars
that I am unable to recover.

"Every time I mention it to him he tells me he will pay
when he has been paid himself. You might also be interested to
hear that he no longer teaches at his college. He is penniless and
out of a job. Please see that I get my money back, and I have the
honor to be (signed): An anxious friend."

For which read: Jarignoux.

I am pleased with my reaction. This "anonymous" mis-
sive now constitutes an indigestible fraction of the equine feces
littering my stable floor. My excessively self-righteous neighbor
is beginning to verge on the comic. I shall have my revenge in
seeing the expression that comes over his face when he learns
from my mouth—or possibly from my hand about his fat face
—that René Leys draws ten thousand taels of the Court budget
monthly . . . And once his appointment as Farmer-General of
the Salt-tax with so many thousand dollars' worth of transit per

day becomes official (for this young man is heading for the top) the Jarignoux' of this world will do well to keep quiet and switch flags once again to cover their greedy carcasses . . .

Supposing, after all, my wretched neighbor really is hard up for cash . . . ?

3 OCTOBER 1911

Early this morning—very early: it was hardly even day, for we are at the beginning of October and the Chinese calendar, once the harvest is in, proclaims an astonishing retardation of custom and the dawn—René Leys was already mounted on his skittish beast, the one he always rides, and I was about to leap into the saddle when my groom, holding the stirrup with one hand, offered me piously in the other a scrap of paper covered in European writing, which he had just extricated from the horse dung.

Not thinking, I unfolded it. Still not thinking, I blushed, and as if to excuse myself to Leys I pocketed the thing with elaborate care . . .

"How extraordinary it is, isn't it—the respect these great-grandchildren of Chinese scholars, even when they are mere servants, have for the written word! Do you know what this good *mafu* has just handed me? An old laundry bill . . . He is quite right, as it happens—it has not been paid yet. It will be."

He passed in front on his strangely aggressive mount, riding out into the gray dawn . . . The sky was manifestly hesitating between the coming winter and the high summer that is drawing to its close. Enter gently the long-drawn-out autumn, the only really settled season of the four, the other three all bursting like cataclysms in blasts of wind, heat, or cold, and proceeding in sustained assaults of dust, incandescence, or ice . . .

This was a really lovely dawn that was unfolding before us, and for the first time I observed that René Leys was touched by a sense of the hour and by the things around us . . . He breathed deeply. A poet would have said without hesitation that "he sighed." He looked up—"at the heavens"—then in front of him—"scanning the horizon"—and he turned to me and smiled. Never have I seen him smile quite like that. He seemed to be groping for something that eluded expression . . .

At length, almost weeping, his dark eyes grown suddenly younger, he said, "What a magnificent morning!"

And I knew that the lad was in love.

He became confidential: "I didn't follow your advice. You told me to say no, didn't you?"

"No to what? The 'Horse Jacket'? Certainly not!"

"No—to the little concubine the Regent had offered me."

"Even less so! But are you still thinking of accepting? This is serious. I mean you'll be letting yourself in for a jealous scene with a vengeance. You won't be able to keep it dark, you know. What will She think about it—the Other Woman?"

And raising my two joined fists I designated Her or Him upon whom the Throne is incumbent.

"I shan't try to keep it dark," was his artless reply. "She has her 'counter-agents' whom she pays never to let me out of their sight. But it is She who made me accept . . ."

"Well, what are you doing prancing about the streets on horseback and talking about it when you ought to be acting?"

"I have."

"At last!"

"Oh, yes—when I left you the day before yesterday it wasn't Her I was going to see . . ."

And the delight in his face told me all I needed to know . . .

"She had wanted to give me a concubine too!" he explained.

"What—She had?"

"Yes. She said it wasn't right that a man of rank should not have a concubine. There are certain days in the month when a concubine is necessary."

"Indeed."

"She offered me one of her ladies-in-waiting . . . She understood about my not finding her . . . acceptable because the Regent had already set aside another one for me."

"So?"

"She let me see her. So I went back to the Regent's palace and offered my concubine a European carriage . . ."

"Is that all?"

"This time she wasn't afraid of me. Besides, I think the Regent had put in a word on my behalf."

I loved the poetry of this politic defloration. Without venturing to recapture the feelings of the young acceptee—by order —I could testify to the fact that those of the acceptor had lent him that "certain something," that air of victory and assurance that comes of a solid conquest . . .

And so our ride went on . . . as sweet as a honeymoon . . . as relaxed as an exchange of confidences . . . on and on . . .

. . . Until his wretched horse started playing up again. The devil shied at every hole. This time, though, there was an excuse—the beast had nearly put his foot down a well! The whole of the Northern Plain is like that—it sucks people down through lipless, rimless mouths that have slaked their thirst . . . Much to my surprise his horse escaped a whipping. Instead he turned to me like a child caught napping and said:

"I'm so sorry—it was my fault. I panicked . . . It's hardly surprising. To think that twelve of my best men have gone down there already!"

With that his face changed. The glad expression in his proud eyes turned tragic. This time it was my turn to be caught napping as he turned to me and asked point blank:

"Will you promise you will execute my will? I shall tell you what I should like to be done in case I die. First, remove the two porcelain basins which Himself gave me from my house.

Then say that I've fallen in the canal . . . or taken the Trans-Siberian . . . Then go to the Bank of China whose address you will find in the right-hand pocket of my jacket and . . ."

Rather tardily I interrupted with a question as to what this was all in aid of . . .

"I'm going to try one last thing," he said. "I told you—the danger now is from the secret societies . . . I've been trying to catch them in the act because they've killed my twelve best agents. They always hold their meetings in Chien Men Wai, and this time I'm going to attend one of them myself . . . in person . . ." He faltered. "If you don't see me again, look for me . . . down some well."

I protested. I had no wish to lose him. Chien Men Wai, I resolved, would be seeing more of me in future.

"Look," I said, "it strikes me you're biting off rather more than you can chew here. Can't I be of some help?"

He thought about this, leaning forward and looking me full in the face, and his decision suddenly hit me as being that of a man . . .

"No, I don't want to involve you . . ."

All right, I thought, but supposing I want to be involved? I did not answer for a long time . . . not until we were back beneath the ramparts, heading for home at a walk, as if we had agreed to be sensible . . .

Then suddenly, spontaneously, I turned on him and called him *tu*:

"You want to gamble with your life? You called me *tu* in your Chinese letter—so let me return the compliment! Listen—never, in China, forget that you are a European."

"I know that!" he reposted. "My mother was French. But I have to disguise myself as a Chinese!"

"Disguise yourself as a Redskin or a Lapp if it's going to help . . . but don't forget—when it comes to the crunch, you still have your transformation scene in hand. You shout at them, 'I'm a foreigner!' "

He gave me a sad smile. "It'll scare them . . . for a minute or two . . . but they'll still strangle me afterwards . . ."

"Yes. This is serious. Where will the meeting take place?"

Confidentially he brought his horse's lips closer to my horse's ears.

"In 'Mutton Bone Alley.' It's a dead end. Near the theatre . . ."

"Good—yes, I know it. I'll be obliged if you can hold out for two minutes at least. But first give a whistle. I won't be far away—I shall be on the alert in the restaurant opposite. I swear that before two minutes are up I shall be beside you in my lounge suit and European hat . . . Your stranglers will be in for a second surprise . . ."

He heard me out, thought it over, and offered me his hand: "All right."

We covered the rest of the way home at a walk, neither of us forcing the pace.

I know the area pretty well, in fact, but I suddenly felt like making a reconnaissance trip. One can never be too sure of one's wells and one's escape routes. I chose the quietest of my horses, intending to use the European sense of humor as a pretext for entering the various inns and gaming houses without dismounting . . .

And so I set out, reconstructing from memory the "knight's progress"—after the knight has indulged in a little too much rose wine—across the intricate and often distorted grid of the Chinese City, which does not, as the chessboard of the Tatar City does, conform to the alignment of the four cardinal points . . . I pretended, as one skilled in police work, to be drunk . . . A European can get in anywhere as long as he pays well. People accept his obligation to indulge in amorous or other intrigue. And a European a bit tight on Chinese alcohol is entitled to every sympathy . . . I received a warm welcome everywhere I went.

Moreover, to make my pretense more effective I really had drunk too much wine . . . rose wine . . . thus granting myself every kind of license, including the poetic. Not that I had the opportunity of indulging any other, I must admit . . . I charged my snorting mount with lowered head at obstacles that were not high so much as highly exiguous in width—namely the thresholds of Chinese houses, which consist of a single plank laid on the floor, but which are framed by two jambs as broad as a naked man. My horse got through, however . . . as did my knees. These obstacles were generally preceded by a flight of four steep steps, which had to be negotiated hoof by hoof—an exercise that my horse performed with the meticulous precision of a circus animal. To my Chinese shame I have to confess that he learned to do so at the Temple of Agriculture. The venerable old peasant in charge of the nine Imperial steps was chortling with joy even before my tip was in his hand . . . I must have been a little drunk that day too, but today I really had no choice.

In this condition of inebriation both assumed and acquired, then, I set out to explore the seedy district of Chien Men Wai with its dubious crossroads and peculiarly Pekingese alleys or *hutung*, some of which go through and others of which are dead ends . . . Dead! But of course, I realized—they must all end in wells! It was a disturbing thought.

As if he understood what was going on, my well-behaved horse suddenly began to balk for no apparent reason. At one point nothing would persuade him to return backwards over the tiny obstacle—one of the plank doorsteps!—that he had just passed with his two front legs and then with his two hind legs . . . He was clearly unaware of the great Taoist principle: "All may be turned end to end; nothing will be changed." Another time he made a mess of negotiating a staircase backwards and very nearly sat down under me. He wasn't drunk enough. Not like I was, for example—on principle!

As I still am, in fact—as it were professionally. For the whole thing has been very much like some kind of enlistment . . . in his Secret Police. Having searched the terrain, I must now search myself . . . turn out the pockets of my heart . . . What made me do it? Was it curiosity? Was it the thrill of discovery? Or was it perhaps a nobler feeling of friendship for this brave young man who was suddenly, that day, for the first time in my presence, afraid, really afraid, because of a well! And even then he was not ridiculous.

No, it was more: it was the desire to know once and for all who and what he is (something he may not even know himself yet)! His luck is extraordinary. If it holds for another year, and if I am lucky enough myself to get him out of some tight spot ... or well ... I shall be close to having my heart's desire: he will introduce me as his best friend to Her ... and the rest is up to court etiquette ... Then at last I shall know what I so deeply desire to know. Then I shall experience what I yearn to experience. That will be my policeman's pay, my recompense; that will be my "Horse Jacket"!

There will be something to get really drunk on. Meanwhile sleep, be it ever so laden with honors, has its demands as well!

He has fully recovered both his nerve and his high spirits. The gloomy pessimism of our last ride together is quite forgotten, and for the last few days he has spoken of nothing but women and flowers and poems given and received, of the beauty of the Pei-king autumn, and of the new friendship that the Regent has shown toward him since he accepted the concubine.

He is cleared of every accusation of the Jarignoux' of this world, for this too-serious young man has at the time of writing two women officially in his arms! And what women! The one experienced, and in the best dynastic tradition. The other barely initiated, ripe for fresh introductions of a procedural and traditional nature . . . Yet it was I who had to steer him back to a sense of the fitting, to get him to speak of his professional duties again, his fears, his will that he mentioned a week ago, his plans, his wells . . .

He replied with an air of mystery—a mystery that I felt had already been cracked and exposed.

"Oh, it's not Chien Men Wai any more—they're *inside* the Palace now."

This struck me as being indeed very much more serious.

"Have you never wondered," he added, "why Pei-king is called Pei-king?"

"No, never."

"It means 'Northern Capital.' But that's not the official name. The administrative district is always referred to as 'Chung-tu Fu.' "

"Yes, I know."

"What do people from the provinces say when they talk about going to Pei-king?"

"That's right—they just say that they're going to the 'Capital.' They never specify that it's the 'Northern Capital.' "

"So where does the name 'Pei-king' come from? Where is it written?"

"I've no idea."

For the first time for over a year it occurred to me to wonder whether the name of this city that I am living in, that I inhabit to a greater extent than any other inhabitant of it, that I am trying to possess, trying to dominate as much as or more than the Emperor himself—it occurred to me to wonder whether this city and its name do in fact have any solid, deep-seated existence other than in legend and history.

He reassured me. "The two characters 'Pei-king' are written down *somewhere* in the city."

"Well—where?"

"In the Imperial City, *under* the road leading from Pei-t'ang to Pei-t'a . . ."

"Oh, I've been along that road . . ."

"Many times. But the first time with me. I took you there. Do you not remember anything unusual about it?"

"No . . ."

But suddenly I did—his horse's incomprehensible shying . . .

"Yes," I was obliged to confess, "your horse's incomprehensible shying . . ."

"You didn't notice . . ."—he paused and smiled—". . . that it sounded hollow? No? That's the place, though. That's the very place where the two characters 'Pei-king,' Northern Capital, are written. I'd better warn you, though—they're not easy to make out. For one thing, in summer you can see nothing at all because the water level is too high."

"What water is that?"

"Did you not feel that just there the road passes over the aqueduct that supplies the Palace?"

"No, I didn't. What about in winter?"

"In winter? In winter it's all frozen up! No one's going to go down there in winter, or if so very carefully, crawling along the ice . . ."

My turn to smash the ice. "I really don't see the connection between this aqueduct and . . ."

"That's how they got in!"

And he proceeded to let me into the secret . . . He had completely mastered his fear. Yet it had been a fine fear, the truest fear there is, the kind the will stiffens itself with! I understood and excused his involved vagaries, realizing that just now he has almost more happiness than he can deal with all at once: his friendship with the Regent, his two loves—one his mistress, one his slave—this danger . . . these thousand, ten thousand dangers to parry and avoid . . .

He let me into the secret—"in depth." Pei-king is not, as one might think, a chessboard whose game, fair or foul, is played on the surface. No—there is an Underground City complete with its redans, its corner forts, its highways and byways, its approaches, its threats, its "horizontal wells" even more formidable than the wells of drinking and other water that yawn up at the open sky . . . He described it all so well that by the time he had finished he had got me trembling myself . . .

He has let me into the secret, and I begin to admire him. He comes and goes in his usual way. Yet for me he has suddenly opened up other Palaces of Dreams whose passages I am far from having trodden! None of this was on my plan of the City! It's—and I can't get away from it; I keep coming back to it in spite of myself—it's as mysterious as the Forbidden City itself! All the unknown, thrice immured behind twenty-foot-high walls, has taken on ten times the mystery in being furnished with this vertical abyss at their base—the Profound City with all its subterranean cavitations! Beneath the broad, flat expanse of the capital anything that even nibbles at the dimension of depth is unexpected . . . disturbing . . .

And his astonishing skill at making his horse rear—that mystic beast straight out of some Mongol apocalypse with a pedigree improvised at the European race meetings sponsored by the Tientsin Bank Co., a prey to the powers of divination that poets and theosophers have (for want of anything better) insisted on attributing to this obtuse animal—his horse, rearing with such apropos on a piece of road that really did sound hollow! I remember the scene. It was just before he took me on that amazing ride when I told him everything. Strange that I should remember it so well: the first day I came across him somewhere other than at my house or at his house, the first day I really *discovered* him . . . yes, it sounded hollow!

Just as I was about to tell him of my admiration for him, my fears, and my suggestions as to possible preventive police measures, he carelessly let drop, "It's all been looked after. I've given orders for the aqueduct to be walled up. I told them the water that came through it was dirty and that the fashion among Europeans now was to drink only 'bottled water' or else rain water that has been boiled and churned in a bowl . . ."

An excellent solution. Hygienic, ingenious, and trebly prudent. Every revolt is thus cut off from its mode of access in advance. The Empire squats solidly upon its own immunity!

11 OCTOBER 1911

Item in the Pekingese paper: "*Revolt in Hupeh province.* The Tenth Division, stationed in Wuchang, has burned down the Viceroy's *yamen*. The Viceroy"—appropriately—"has fled. The rebels have seized control of the artillery and are bombarding the forts of Hanyang. There is some alarm among the European concessions in Hankow . . ."

These three cities—or rather this Triple City, far too well known in Europe by the character of umbilical center of China conferred upon it, with its five gratuitous millions of inhabitants, by Wells' *Anticipations*—these three cities are indeed, whether one like it or not, places to be reckoned with in Chinese politics. The revolt, moreover, is of the "military" kind with magazine-fed rifles and artillery . . . More seriously even than de la Rochefoucauld-Liancourt meant—this is a revolution!

But there can't be a "revolution" in China—even a rebellion is barely possible! I must have a word with René Leys about it. He is the only person who can tell me how important this mutiny really is. He alone will be directly involved if they turn their attention to the dynastic incumbents of the Throne. After all, as chief of the secret police and lover of the Empress he alone—I shall tell him—is doubly, or is it decuply, paid for that purpose.

Later I did not ask questions. I decided to wait for him to give me his opinion on the matter. His manner when he arrived was deeply mysterious. He was much less concerned with a particular European date, 11 October 1911—my *fête,* apparently, the name day of my thirty-fifth year—than with celebrating this anniversary in the Chinese fashion. He meant me to have my "show" not at the theatre but in my own home. He was delighted with his idea. He promised me actors of the first—*i.e.* highest paid—class, and told me the title of the play: *The Meeting in the Mulberry Orchard.* He had already given my servants something to put up a stage against the west wall of my courtyard. He left again, bubbling over with a genuine gaiety such as I have not seen him betray so overtly for a long time.

Two hours later he was back, preceded by a quartet of musicians with the two-stringed violin, the clappers, that emperor of every orchestra, the gong, and a solemn-sounding pipe used for the entrances of princes. He brought up the rear, accompanied by "his" friends.

I was pleased to see them again. The "Big Bespectacled Fellow" was there, and the Nth Nephew of the whichever-it-is of our Princes . . . But the whole troupe had already disappeared inside a lean-to which usually serves as my harness shed. After a few moments the orchestra, which had installed itself at the back of the stage, began to tune up in a din of discordant sound. And before I fully realized what was happening the "show" was under way—with me as the only spectator! It was about . . . This time I knew what it was about: René Leys and his troupe . . . A breakthrough in police organization, no doubt . . . They performed evolutions, they pirouetted, they acted with quite professional precision. Here again there were fights—but compulsory ones—entries, reprises, mistakes—but these on principle. Thanks to my well-remembered initiation, I knew exactly to the instant when I ought to applaud, and I launched energetically into a series of those guttural "Rrrroow!" sounds that here do duty for all the claps of the Parisian and the whistles of the American audience.

I thought it was really nice of him to lay on this piece of "theatre in the home" for me and did not stint my "Rrrroows."

When he joined me again—modest, his makeup removed, perspiring slightly, proud and pleased with himself—I knew I ought first to compliment him . . . but there was something or other that had displeased, even disconcerted me . . . Why should I hide my feelings from him, I thought. So I told him: something a bit histrionic, and more than a little phony—particularly in China—had displeased me about his performance.

He answered with complete self-assurance, "She is so fond of the theatre, you see! She made me promise to learn this part. You tell me I played it well for you—that's all I wanted to hear. But I've got to play it for Her . . . the day after tomorrow."

For Her? Most indiscreetly I repeated aloud, "For Her . . . ? But which one? Whom do you mean?"

"My 'Number One,' " he said. "There is nothing my 'number two' can ask of me."

Oh happy and victorious young man who must thus enumerate his loves! Long live polygamy amid the highest and holiest functions of State! I should never have imagined its Imperial factors reduced to mere arithmetic. And yet René Leys was right. Decency demands that the young concubine of the Regent's gift, accepted and possessed, duly remain "number two" in this new system of accounting.

And I seriously wanted to take him to task, to reduce him to a common denominator, to common factors . . . but revolutionary ones! What, I wanted to know, did the Palace think of the events taking place now, in our time, in the triple city of Wuchang, Hanyang, and Hankow?

But with a spring in his step he left me, having lowered the curtain on the show. (A gesture for which there is no equivalent in the language of the Chinese theatre.) He was aware that he had "played his part well," *for me*. He was confident he could now play it without nervousness for Her. He left me, a satisfied spring in his step.

All the rest—the revolt on the Yangtze exactly a thousand

kilometers to the south of here—seems rather far away, and, seen from here, in the middle of my courtyard with its memory of the elegant mannerisms of the theatre, rather . . . provincial.

13 OCTOBER 1911

I really must see him—and without any theatre this time. Things are going very badly for his friends, the Dynastic Manchus. I hope that the extreme south—that almost tropical colony of Kwangtung which Sun Yat-sen has been agitating and clumsily trying to raise—will hold true . . . but all the towns of the center are in an uproar. The whole valley of the mighty Yangtze from Tibet to the sea and all the cities dotted along its course are "buzzing and swarming like hives of bees," to use a simile well worn already by four hundred years of Chinese historical literature.

I did in fact see him—or rather caught a glimpse of him —as he was climbing into a carriage sent specially for him by the Imperial spectatrix . . . He was already costumed—very well costumed, too—as a Manchu princess, but he also had with him the "Horse Jacket," his pretext, his palladium, that *zaïmph* that is supposed to ensure him every entrée—whether great or small —and secure him, like some Matho, safe passage wherever he goes . . .[9] I barely had time to catch his reassuring reply:

"Don't worry about a thing! We've just dispatched a good half brigade of Imperial troops for Hankow. They'll never hold out against them. And above all don't talk about revolution. What we're dealing with here is a rebellion."

It strikes me that something similar—only the other way round—was said some hundred and twenty years ago, and in a pretty ominous context![10]

After all, I thought, as I went out this evening, I have promised to help him. I am involved in his game. I have taken sides—the side of our Manchus with their Fine Forbidden Cities. And I am observing the rules of the game, studying in advance the progress of each of its pawns.

Winter was in the air, and how cold and desolate everything felt all of a sudden! Yet for Himself's sake and for our side I sallied forth for Chien Men Wai, which comprises not only the districts catering to drunkenness and pleasure but also the Main Station, terminus of the Franco-Belgian-Chinese railway line "Hankow-Peking"! I wanted to see at firsthand the mobilization of the Imperial troops, those loyal soldiers who will shortly, by order, have defeated the "Rebels."

The Great Gate was indeed crowded with gunners trying to catch up with their guns and swarms of coolies struggling to load the ammunition wagons. This was the "half-brigade" that was being dispatched to the depths of the provinces to uphold both Throne and Altar. These people were going off to war, yet how gay, inoffensive, and clumsy they seemed!

Suddenly their somewhat wobbly ranks were broken by a joyful band coming through the Gate from the Tatar City and heading in the direction of Chien Men Wai . . . where, I thought, they would doubtless soon be staggering drunkenly from tea-house door to teahouse door! But ye Gods of War! And you too, bearded Kuan Ti! If it wasn't that charming company of well-bred young men whose acquaintanceship I owe to René Leys—and the latter in person in their midst!

It occurred to me then that, of course, he had come as I had, cunningly providing himself with an escort, to view the entrainment of the troops . . .

But no. Taking me very mysteriously by my European sleeve he said, "Imagine—we nearly sent them off to the wrong place! It's not the mutiny in Wuchang that's most urgent . . . Do you know what I've just found out here in Pei-king . . . in the 'dead end' to the south of Liu-li Chang . . . ?"

It was more than I could take. What he had "found out" was really a bit too tame for these momentous days. Apparently there has been a resurgence of the "reformist" movement launched by Kang Yu-wei—Kuang Hsu's former adviser—and according to Leys two thousand students, armed with his teachings, are on the march to scour the country around Pei-king.

No really—this I simply could not take . . . It was a case, I decided, either of sudden political blindness—a kind of ostrich reaction—or of deliberate mystification of a kind I wanted no part in.

"And what about the two telegrams from Canton that the European Legations have just received?" I asked somewhat roughly. "I saw them myself. The secretary said nothing about them being secret. The consuls down there say quite independently of all Chinese news sources that the three provinces have declared themselves a republic. They may not have many actual soldiers but they have leaders, and hostages, and quite a bit of money . . ."

René Leys retired into the supremely dignified silence that heralds major confessions.

"Well?" I insisted. "What does he think about that, then—your friend Chun, son of the Seventh Prince and Regent of the Empire?"

He had to reply, "The Regent knows nothing about it yet. No one has dared tell him. The appropriate orders have been given. The War Minister has left for the front . . ."

I was relieved to hear it. So orders had been given; regular troops, regularly paid, were on their way southward.

It was one of those lovely late-autumn evenings . . . Why, after all, should I worry about this exotic Sun Yat-sen, a man as much a "nigger" to the noble Wei Chinese and the pale conqueror from Manchuria as an Ouolof-Arab half-breed stirring up trouble in Dakar when, say, the seat of empire was Dunkerque and its incumbent a fair-haired Viking!

And why, I wondered, was René Leys, who ought to have been at his desk in the Central Bureau of the Secret Police, or in bed if it was his night off, or in other beds than his own . . . why was René Leys to be found at liberty in this very place to which his police turn a blind eye?

But the moment to ask him had passed. We were being jostled by soldiers again, now streaming from the station back into the City. They were no longer leaving. They were going back to their barracks. And in the calm after the storm I have begun to wonder whether our consuls down there were not perhaps exaggerating, whether it is not yet another case of Europeans making their usual mistake and magnifying out of all proportion one of those periodic riots that China swallows, digests, and eliminates with a belch like some vast intestine venting its flatulent rumblings.

This time I felt I really must get in touch with him. This time I meant to force an explanation out of him: once and for all, are your friends their Imperial Highnesses fools to be treated as such, setting everything up for a first-class "fall"—or is it that they have had their fill of Empire and are preparing to retire against a guaranteed pension—or is it, better still, that Empire and Palace and all are but a historian's dream, and everything I have written on the subject but smoke playing upon the dross of nonsense?

Yes—this time, I decided, I absolutely have to see him. Had I had that precious pink handkerchief in my pocket, that "passport" that opens almost every door, I should have used it as my magic wand in search of this man whose ubiquity, I realized, was beginning to alarm me. Just then when I wanted him, where was he? Certainly not under the paternal roof! Nor at his College, either, for it was closed in the first few days of the disturbances for lack of students, most of the noblemen's sons having gone over to the "revolution." Nor was he in Chien Men Wai—at least not in the more respectable houses I had visited in his company (for I checked) . . . Was he perhaps at the Palace, I wondered. In the Palace? Under the Palace? Nowhere? Vanished into thin air? Spirited away like a sage who has said enough and whose days are numbered? I was prepared for any eventuality...

...but certainly not to come home and find him peacefully waiting for me, his serene, everyday self. I was beside myself...

"You're making a fine mess of things at the Palace!"

He assumed an air of innocence.

"Do you know who's just been appointed Viceroy of the Two Hu," I ranted on, "with the country in revolt?"

"But I told you the War Minister ... had left ..."

"A fig for your War Minister! He'll never make it. Not with the colleague they've just given him!"

His coolness, his silence, his whole attitude of reserve were beginning to put me off my stroke.

"They've just appointed ..." I got out ... and then I gave it to him, the Regent's decree of yesterday appointing Yuan Shih-kai—the exile in retirement on his country estate—Viceroy of the rebellious central provinces of Hunan and Hupeh, Generalissimo of the army and navy, prop to the threatened dynasty!

"You're mad—all of you!" I went on. "What makes the Regent think that the man he practically beheaded three years ago is going to come back and serve under him! The Old Fox didn't just step down in disgrace without preparing his comeback. But what a comeback! He has his soldiers—five or six thousand Honan men. He has his bodyguard—well armed, well paid, and well drilled. And he has his whole province behind him—Honan, quintessence of the 'Middle Flower.'"

But René Leys brought me back to a less poetic appraisal of the situation.

"Oh—Yuan's appointment," he offered nonchalantly. "Yes—I suggested that."

He looked me in the eye. "It was the best way of keeping him away from Pei-king, where he might have been a nuisance just now. He's a good soldier. Let him get himself killed somewhere else."

His tone of voice, his look, his phrasing, all were so decisive that I could not but bow to them. These Manchus really are the most astute politicians—and René Leys the nimblest of their jugglers.

Today, though, he came back looking pretty worried.

"Could you look after some money for me?"

"No trouble at all. But the European banks . . ."

"I don't want to be recognized! I'd rather hand this over to you . . . It's all I've been able to save from bankruptcy."

All he'd been able to save! That was already too much, I thought—if it was but a tithe I should find myself responsible for an impressive sum.

He handed me a bulky Chinese envelope of blue-flowered paper and extracted from his pocket a heavy packet wrapped up in the famous pink silk handkerchief.

"All right," I said, "I'll give you a receipt. What figure shall I put?"

He insisted we count it again together. There were forty-eight silver dollars—Che-li piastres—and twenty-eight five-dollar bills of the "Hong Kong and Shanghai Bank" of which fifteen were "Tientsin issue" and thirteen "Pei-king issue." A hundred and eighty-eight dollars in all. Just about four hundred francs.

And this was *all* that remained of his stupendous salary! These sapeke were the sole survivors . . . of what astronomical bankruptcy . . . ?

My rudely disillusioned air forced him into explanations. It had happened the night before: the news of the rebellion of the central provinces had reached the point where all the Shanghai banks had crashed . . .

"You mean you gave them . . ."

"Not them, no—their Pei-king subsidiaries. Listen—they were giving me twenty-four per cent per annum!"

"And the Pei-king banks went too? But couldn't you have . . . anticipated it . . . even by a day? Just time enough to . . . I mean . . . what's your police force for?"

"I knew before anyone," he answered. And his eyes flashed with the pride of his finest hours as he said, "It was I that was ordered to announce the crash and arrest the bankers."

"Have you done so?"

"This very night. Five of my men and myself . . . There was some fighting . . ."

"And you lost all you had?"

"And got a pretty good kick in the stomach. It still hurts . . ."

He rubbed his stomach and his eyes glazed over, the pupils swiveling upward. He almost fell. Recovering himself, he said, "Ah well, here we go again!"

He refused to lie down and relax with an ice pack on his belly—the recommended treatment in such cases, I believe. No —off he went with a nonchalant air, almost refusing the receipt I offered him.

I have just bumped into the fat laugh and even fatter face of my neighbor Jarignoux at the corner of my street, or rather our street. I could not turn my back on him—that would have been to flee and leave him the field—nor was there any chance of his not hailing me jovially as I passed . . . Besides, I very much wanted to know how he would take my handing him back his letter, the somewhat soiled letter that, after disinfection, I had placed in my pocket against just such a joyful encounter as this. With meticulous care I unfolded it for him.

"Ah—kept it, did you? Not very wise. I took the liberty of not compromising myself. You might have found it awkward to talk to me about it. But you can tear it up now. And thanks for jogging the youngster's memory—he paid me back a couple of days later."

Then, in an access of good humor, he added, "He may have had a tough time of it. The boy's broke. Spent all he had left of his salary on girls and there'll not be any more because the College is closed. Won't be opening again all that soon, either, thanks to our Socialist comrades in Canton! All his students have already made off for Wuchang as apprentice revolutionaries. And now they're saying 'Father Yuan' is heading for Pei-king. I wouldn't give a piastre for the Regent's aristocratic skin! Pleasure to see a fine country—and a rich one—making way for the beacons of progress!"

With unconcealed scorn I crumpled and tore up the letter that had occasioned this interview and took my leave of him for what I believe to have been the last time. For a future Chinese voter he seems to be pretty poorly informed on the subject of the political significance of Yuan's recall. "We are perfectly aware"—and despite myself I can hear the habitually confident timbre of Leys' voice—"We are perfectly aware that We have ordered him to take up his appointment at the head of the provincial troops as quickly as possible in order to keep him away from the Capital . . ."

Yuan Shih-kai heading for Pei-king . . . Another tall story by this naturalized Chinese punting on his career and anxious to gather his scheming wiles about him!

Something new at last among the Manchu caste! Master Wang, whom I had not seen for two months—policeman's holiday—called to see me today. He spoke in whispers and his dear old face looked very, very frightened. Apparently they are in a terrible panic at the Palace, although they are far from clear in their minds exactly what about. Ought they to be more frightened that Sun Yat-sen will suddenly steam up the Imperial Canal from Hankow to Tientsin in a Japanese warship, or that some perpetual descendant of the Ming will have himself consecrated emperor in Nan-king? They are also afraid that Mongolia will take its tribute to Russia, that the French will divide Yünnan up into *départements,* and that the frozen rivers of the north will start to thaw! Signs have been seen in the sky—a headless dragon sporting a black felt hat in the shape of a watermelon, a yellow tortoise wearing a European suit instead of a shell. The traditional measures are being put in hand: the Imperial Guard has been given two months' back pay, three hundred eunuchs have been laid off, the Regent's Princess Consort is packing her bags and wants to flee . . . but has still to decide where to—Jehol, probably, in the Northern Mountains: that is the usual bolt-hole in all major catastrophes.

"What about yourself, Master Wang?" I asked.

Master Wang said he did not wish to flee but simply to move to another house. He gradually brought me to see how, in case of a riot in Pei-king, his life and person, deeply compromised by the hair style and race of his lady wife, would be most agreeably secure were they under my roof. Oh—the merest lodging in one of my outbuildings!

I was embarrassed, having really only one part of my house that I could spare—the southern part.

"It's the room where Mr. 'Lei' stays, you see . . . although it's true he doesn't use it much any more."

And for a moment I contemplated asking René Leys if he would mind my housing in his stead a couple who were in infinitely greater danger than himself . . . until I realized that he is in a more exposed position than anyone: the chief of the secret police, unless he resigns or disappears in time, is the first to forfeit his person in these anti-dynastic affairs. The perhaps imaginary or exaggerated risks that he has told me about—that he is so frightened about—are nothing to the risks one can think of . . . I was sure that Master Wang, an S.P. man himself, would understand.

I explained. I said I was sorry but that Mr. Lei's "high office" made things very risky for him just at present and that I was anxious to keep this refuge available for him in my house.

Master Wang expressed some surprise at this.

"But a European has nothing to fear, even if he is a Professor at the College of Nobles!"

"I meant his high office in . . . the Secret Police . . ."

At a time when everyone on "our" side must stand up and be counted, I thought, there is no point in keeping one's counsel. So I apprised Master Wang, the humble subordinate, of the more recent of René Leys' official titles and one or two of his more avowable exploits.

Master Wang said he knew nothing of all this. There had been a foreigner in "the service," he admitted, but in a lower grade. A German. He had been convicted of theft and given the sack. The present chief was a Pekingese by the name of Siu.

Master Wang, I realized, is an excellent policeman himself—secretive, discreet, not at all the sort to give away his superiors, even to me. If he but knew that I know everything—and, like the Phoenix, much more besides!

We agreed that he should have a little nook which he discovered himself behind my western building, an extension I did not even know I had. He and his wife would install themselves there, he assured me, without compromising us in the least.

Before he left I asked him what his Manchu friends think of the return to favor of the Chinese Yuan Shi-kai?

Nothing. They think nothing. It passed unremarked among the daily appointments. He is now fighting in the war down in the south. When that has been cleared up he will be given some token of official gratitude.

I did not even have time to fetch René Leys. From the rush of cheering people in the Street of the Legations I learned that "He's coming" and that "He'll be here in ten minutes"; also that trouble was expected, and that no one was sure whether the whole of Pei-king might not be in flames before nightfall.

It was an historic moment, I realized. The Old Fox has played his cards well. A secretary from the Russian Legation told me all the details as we ran to the station together—the game of offer and refusal that he played so superbly and has brought to such a triumphant conclusion, and not one echo of which penetrated as far as my Chinese quarter whereas every other foreigner in Pei-king has been charting its moves for the last ten days. Here it is: the disgraced and exiled Yuan Shih-kai, suddenly appointed Viceroy of the Two Hu, very shrewdly turned down the appointment on medical grounds (his leg was still bad). Whereupon he was appointed not Viceroy but Generalissimo of the troops being dispatched against the rebels. He accepted, and stayed where he was. On being enjoined to take up his appointment at the front, a few leagues from Hankow and a thousand kilometers south of Pei-king, he quickly raised all the troops he could command and set out—but northwards, in the direction of the Capital . . . And now he was almost here

. . . Another ten minutes . . . We decided we should have a good view of his arrival from the top of the ramparts. We ran and ran, and were in time!

The first train was very much longer than the platform. About a thousand soldiers alighted—well-fed peasants with round, red faces. The second train contained the same. Then nothing more for two hours . . .

It was dark before the last convoy arrived—valets, guards, women, old-style soldiers brandishing fearsome halberds and forming a dense, moving hedge around a brisk little man with unforgettably powerful eyes that swept the ramparts on which I was perched and took in the whole city at a glance, this city he was now entering as master without a siege, as servant a hundred times stronger than the lord who had appointed him. He was wearing the yellow robe, the "Horse Jacket," and the winter hat with the pheasant's feather. A second glance—a very mild, very friendly one—for the Europeans who have never looked to him in vain and who had gathered to cheer him in . . . and he was almost carried by his guards to the waiting Berlin with the huge black horses—rather too Russian-looking, the horses, in the ancient Chinese context of the moment . . . The guards ran alongside and leapt on the footboards, and the equipage moved off at a spanking pace through . . . the *side* gate, the one the common people use every day when they get off the train and enter the demilune of Chien Men.

Although so sure of himself already he had the patience, the modesty not to demand that the imperially sealed south doors be opened for him. He has a sense of how to place each of his gestures in their proper order. He drove off in comfort on his European springs to take up residence, like a good paterfamilias, in the well-fortified *yamen* of his eldest son Yuan Ko-ting.

I was dying to tell René Leys about it all, for much to my surprise I had not seen him among the crowd coming down from the ramparts afterwards. Yet when I got home it seemed the most natural thing in the world to find him sitting, rested

and refreshed, in the room where he told me he had slept the
whole afternoon—"better than I have slept for a long time." He
was afraid the kick he had received "might have smashed a
nerve in my bladder—but it doesn't hurt any more down here
and I'm urinating . . ."

I cut him short. Did he take me for a doctor? It was indecent. I was ashamed for my still-ardent enthusiasm and resolved not to mention Yuan's splendid arrival for the moment.
I said nothing.

"Well?" he challenged me. "You were convinced we'd
never get him to leave, weren't you?"

". . . ?"

"He's left."

"Left and arrived. I know. I've . . ."

"Yes, arrived at his post."

"Ah?"

"I'm pleased with myself for insisting he be sent down
there. The Regent refused to believe we'd be rid of him so
easily . . ."

"Ah!"

"Now he's up against the Revolutionaries with their
twenty or forty thousand men. He'll have his work cut out for
him. He could have been dangerous in the North, I'll admit . . .
Don't tell anyone this, but I was there when the confidential dispatches from Hankow were opened—he is precisely ten kilometers from there . . . and that makes him a thousand from Pei-
king . . ."

I stared at René Leys with a frankness I never knew my
face was capable of. His own calm made me quite calm, yet it
still seems prodigious that I was able to come out with it:

"What have you been doing today? Have you been drinking or something? Are you ill? Have you had a letter from your
father?"

His face in turn became a picture of frank amazement.

"Well, listen," I explained, "I haven't had any confidential dispatches myself but I'm going to tell you under the seal of

absolute secrecy that Yuan Shih-kai is within these walls . . ."

His expression became wooden.

"You must swear," I added with a slightly bitter laugh, "not to breathe a word of this to the five hundred people who saw him arrive at the station just now . . ."

"At the station?" René Leys asked, somewhat disconcerted. "By what train? What time was this?"

"I'm telling you—just now."

"Impossible."

"But I was there!"

And I described the scene: the two train loads of soldiers, the guards, the crowd . . . the Europeans, whom there is no deceiving . . .

He said nothing. For the first time I had the feeling that he was searching for what he intended to tell me. I fell silent too . . . Now it was I that was disconcerted . . .

With some difficulty (was it the dry irritation of this winter that has already begun?—there was something of a crackle in my voice) I went on, "Look—you can tell me what you like about your personal friends but let me tell you what I *know*. I know enough about 'Father Yuan' to be able to tell you I saw him get off that special train, the third one to arrive, at seven p.m. by the European clock, climb into a carriage (drawn by two black horses), enter Pei-king by the west gate, and drive through Chien Men . . . and disappear . . ."

"You say you saw someone . . . climb into a carriage?" His voice was authoritative. "It wasn't him."

"What!"

"I'm going to tell you something very, very important. You'll be the only person who knows this apart from the Regent and myself . . ."

I stared at him. I realized I had hurt him. He was paler than I have ever seen him before . . .

"Tell me," I said, to console him.

"Old Yuan is in Pei-king, I grant you. But I was right when I said you didn't see him climbing into a carriage. That wasn't him. That was his double, the man that stands in for him on official occasions to be on the safe side. The real Yuan has been here since . . . since . . ."

All right, damn it, I thought—let him faint, then! Let him throw one of his fits. Let's get it over with. The joke was becoming too tense for me. I had wanted him to feel some of the tension . . .

Too late. All I had before me was a child, sitting in an armchair, his head thrown back, his eyes turned up in their sockets, his lips like chalk . . . I knew it would last ten minutes, and that it happens to him after various emotional shocks. What was today's, I wondered. Yuan's arrival in flesh and blood, even if in the person of his double, or resentment at not being believed in so unbelievable a story?

I decided it was perhaps time to bring him around. A few pats on the hand, a wet towel on his face, and that was it . . .

Discreetly I left him to make his own way back to the real world.

He broached the subject of last night's episode himself today, asking me in some embarrassment, "Is that the first time you've seen me faint?"

"No. The third."

He was very shaken by this and proceeded to confess to me that "other things are beginning to alarm him" because at "times like those" he knows neither who nor where he is.

Choosing his words carefully, he described to me a most curious condition of visual transposition, unexampled in my experience. For instance, when he is out riding in a particular part of Pei-king—say in a street in the southwestern corner—he is suddenly overwhelmed by the certainty that he can actually see before him, but in a reversed mirror image, the corresponding point of the city lying diagonally opposite—i.e. in this case a street in the northwestern corner. Nor is that all: he can ride about as he pleases in the (geometrically) "other" place for as long as he keeps his eyes open and does not blink. He must also hold his breath. The really original detail is that all his movements are subject to the same diagonal transposition: he turns right when he wants to turn left . . . All this happens when he is least expecting it . . . nor is he able to provoke these "visions" at will . . . Sometimes he has as many as three or four in a day, which gets pretty tiring.

In all innocence, almost with affection, I asked, "Your visits to the Palace aren't a little . . . influenced by these visions, are they?"

He continued searching for words, withdrawn into himself, groping for "memories" . . .

"I begin to understand why I'm so afraid of going up on the walls or climbing the towers . . ."

"Why?"

"Because . . . on one occasion this thing came over me and of course I saw myself drowning at the bottom of a . . ."

Of course. Suddenly I saw it myself. In these strange, private moments he lives in a space turned upside down, full of agonizing experiences of penetrating solid matter or of having the law of gravity reversed . . .

Others will say—imaginary agonizing experiences. Possibly. It is possible that he is playing some contemptible game of fabrication . . . of subject and story . . . I feel and maintain, though, that, even as he is talking to me, even as he is confiding in me, he is actually living that anguish, and living it with enviable, almost frightening intensity . . . But I would give a lot to know.

"Have you had visions of this kind inside the Palace itself?" I asked, prompted by my curiosity.

"No."

He let out a dreadful, mechanical sigh. His breathing was labored . . . It occurred to me that these alarms were doing his adolescent heart no good—his physical heart—that they were straining that hollow muscle! It was time, I felt, to return to more solid and less vertiginous subjects, to more familiar territory . . .

"How long is it now," I asked, "since you saw Her last?"

"The day before yesterday. No—three nights."

"Oh, by the way . . . this is a delicate matter, I know . . . but if your 'First Night' was so expensive . . ."

"I know—six thousand dollars . . ."

"I'm sorry—four thousand . . . I have the receipt in my pocket! But how do you manage to raise the amount, now that your College is closed and the banks . . . ? No, I'm only joking . . . Incidentally I am entirely at your service, you know . . . Not that you should have to stop halfway . . . If there's anything I can do for you . . . somewhere to hide, safekeeping for anything you particularly value . . . ?"

"No. The eunuchs know I've lost all I had. I give them promissory notes against my future salary . . . Still, if I ever should need anyone's help, I shall turn to you . . . you can be sure of that. You don't need to tell me twice. If I have anything valuable I want hidden I shall bring it here . . . I have already done so once . . ."

True. What better promise could one have?

Same evening He has gone out, and suddenly I find myself in the most dreadful quandary.

I have known this lad for less than a year. He has told me all about himself, all these stories. I have not said a word to a soul about any of it. I have savored the development, the "feel" of it all without the slightest doubt as to its reality.

But today—only today?—I come to doubt something . . . that is to say, at one swoop I doubt it all.

Moreover, the one state is as unwarranted as the other. There is the same element of brute credence in believing it all as in rejecting it all. I have tried to pull myself together. I tell myself one should not be afraid of the miraculous side of the whole adventure. One should not turn one's back on the mysterious and the unknown. The rare moments in which myth consents to take one by the throat . . . to demand admission among the everyday facts of existence . . . Those hallucinated minutes that can yet be timed with a watch . . . and the reverberations of which subsequently echo over years . . . All these things must be taken into account . . .

The fact remains: the fellow has told me some mysterious

and wonderful stories. No—one story. He has shown me, led me, opened up for me . . . Ah—now I think (I haven't thought of it for a long time) of his Chinese name: he really did open for me down the long nights of this summer and autumn the jade latch of the "Mysterious Garden" of which he seemed to be the master . . . He told it all so well! So many might envy him!

Today, though, by a habit of logic—be it worldly or philosophical—I simply must try and distinguish the *true* from the false . . . the possible from the probable . . . the credible from the disconcerting. Let us assume for the moment that there is some truth in it but that in the boastfulness of youth he may have embellished a few details.

Let us draw up an account. On the one side, his story:

A young Belgian, son of a Belgian grocer (but of a pure-French mother—his insistance on this point is absolute) arrives in China before the age of puberty. He learns a language, known to be a difficult one. He finds his way into the Palace, known to be hermetically sealed. He becomes the chief of a secret organization, the friend of the Regent, the lover of the Dowager, and the only European adviser to the Empire of the "Sons of Heaven" in the most critical moment of its entire existence since the first enthronement!

On the other side, his gifts:

A peculiar aptitude for learning any language composed of imitated sounds, and for taking up any idea that is thrust upon or suggested to him . . . A fervency, an impulsiveness, a certain adolescent beauty; an obvious attractiveness to—and attraction for—women . . .

The account seems to balance pretty well . . . Or, if this is a trial, it seems to be one in which the defense has an answer for everything.

You will reproach me with being too credulous. But I say no. I have conceded already that certain adventures have been sweetened, accentuated, stripped of all possible snags . . . but surely tnat is part of the storyteller's job! And on the other hand how many episodes, how many of his phrases can only

have been the product of "firsthand experience," and as such
worthy not only of the Prix Goncourt but also of the plaudits of
the Human-Document School!

One does not invent such details, such glimpses, such
flashes as . . .

What one can see from the top of the Hill of Contemplation. The Regent's clumsy handshake, which consists of grasp-
ing the thumb and leaving the fingers free. The same Regent's
fear of the danger escaped. The historic account of the Imperial
Wedding Night . . . All the things that are stamped so clearly,
like a graven seal, upon the memory of those days!

No—René Leys must have lived this extraordinary existence . . . And in any case the choice before me is simple: either
I accuse him in my private court, behind his back, like some
anonymous Jarignoux (and suddenly I find my mind is already
made up) or I tell him to his face, in a moment of deepest confidence, all the doubts—ridiculous, clumsy, or over-percipient—
that have assailed me today on his account.

My mind is made up, then: confidence it shall be.

Things are going from bad to worse. The Empire is in *extremis*, with the knife at its throat. The Regent of tomorrow, the rising Regent, Yuan Shih-kai, has respectfully informed the Regent of today, Prince Chun, soon to be of yesterday, that he must abdicate, or rather that he must have abdicated before tomorrow's sun is up. Tonight, then, will be the night of the great debate—perhaps of the great battle: the five thousand Honanese in old Yuan's pay, reinforced by all the (also paid) miscontents in Peiking, will besiege the Palace defended by the Imperial Guard, the S.P., and the plucky little René at their head. There will be fighting both ancient and modern, with mighty shouts and fearful grimaces . . . and Mauser rifles as well. For all my loyalty to their cause, the Manchus will be defeated. And subsequently the Palace will be sacked. Two hundred concubines, most of them ladies of great respectability since they go back to the bed and the reign of the Emperor who was contemporary with our Second Empire, will plead for their lives and surrender to their conquerors. The eunuchs will strive to obtain similar favors. A few bold throwbacks to a bygone age will elect to fight . . . and will be routed, repulsed, and ultimately driven . . .

　　The sequel I cannot get out of my head. We have discussed it already, he and I. He pointed out to me that, in all the sieges of the Forbidden City, the final massacre has always taken place in the four corners.

"You see," he explained, "they're the points farthest away from the gates."

"Of course . . . One need only glance at the plan."

"Ah, the plan!" sighed René Leys, no doubt realizing that, if there is a massacre, it is at one of those four corners that he will fall . . .

But does he not know of any "exit"? How am I going to get him out of this? In terms of honor, his place is certainly there.

Same day, evening   It was a pleasant relief to see him turn up here just before nightfall—the last before the Big Night. The plight of the Dynasty and his preparations notwithstanding, he generously consented to dine with me. We dined—he with an excellent appetite. I was glad for him. The meal, I thought, would do him good. We rose from the table and stretched our limbs. It was a bitter winter night, I reminded him. He would have to dress warmly. Had he his fur? I rang for my boy to bring his things, anxious that he should not be cold. Time enough for that! And I was about to open my mouth to re-offer my services (for this night of all nights) when he forestalled me.

"I'm not going out."

He settled himself in the same chair, in the same comfort, but made more intimate by eight months of confidences, and by the winter cosiness of my house. He was not going out. He was not going to the Palace. I hinted at how much his presence here beside me reassured me. Here he had nothing to fear, I told him, in spite of his police connections, "beneath the folds of the foreign flag" flapping above my gate and lit, as if it were the blood of the lamb to shield us from the massacre, by an ancient, tricolor Chinese lantern! But what about Her! What had She said at his last audience? When had he last seen Her?

Coming out of that now familiar state of dream he stretched himself . . . and said nothing. Then, abruptly: "Supposing . . . She were to come tonight and ask you to hide Her?"

Here was a fine thing! It was said with such directness that I was tempted to take him at his word. Good—let her come . . . tonight . . . this evening . . . now . . . this second! Would she be coming alone? I asked. And the Regent—why not? And . . . the little Emperor? A European household in a Chinese district would certainly be more discreet from the diplomatic point of view than seeking asylum in one of the ten Foreign Legations, among which she would have to make an official choice . . .

"So we can expect Her this evening some time?"

With the same straightforwardness he said, "I came to make sure everything was ready to receive Her."

To receive Her . . . What—just like that? Well, as the Chinese would put it, "my house is far from large but she shall be made most welcome . . ." We'll cope somehow, I thought. My chief boy always copes. I'd better give up my room for a start . . .

He guessed my thoughts. "Oh, she won't be here before the third watch. The attack on the Palace will begin at the fourth." (This for reasons of a . . . strategic nature . . .)

He was his usual self—well-informed and to the point. The third watch would be twelve o'clock midnight. It was not yet eight. And in any case, I thought, surely in these riotous times my Imperial Guest will be indulgent toward the filthy little silkworm who will receive Her in his wretched cocoon . . . (Which is the polite way of putting it.)

"Well, Leys," I said, "until then we can chat just like old times."

"Yes. But I shall be receiving a message from Her, which will mean I shall have to leave for a moment."

"Of course—I quite understand. Feel entirely free, and show Her in yourself, will you? And this message—will it take the form of . . . ? Would you like me to have a quiet word with the gatekeeper?"

"No. It will take the form of an S.P. messenger who will ask to see me and will give me a silk handkerchief."

"A pink one?"

He was suddenly offended. "Certainly not! A yellow one."

"Ah—I'm sorry. Yes, of course, I was forgetting. This one is not from Chien Men Wai."

He appeared calm. Why should calm have eluded me? It has been many evenings since we were able to lie out beneath the sky . . . Now one must remain indoors, in these warm rooms, flinging the door wide occasionally and taking joyful gulps of the icy air that comes rushing in . . .

Was it just that? The words came with difficulty, the atmosphere of confidence was gone . . . He for his part tried instinctively to draw me back; he spoke of his concubine (what would happen to her tonight!), of his grandiose, his "imperial" plans for when the Ch'ing "have consolidated their position again" after the crisis. Verily, verily, I said to myself, his voice is as it has always been these last six months, but the ears that hear it are by no means the same . . .

In fact I was listening for something else. He had said his message would arrive "before the second watch." I was waiting, with much greater impatience than he, for another message. I was waiting—and there was not a movement in the icy air outside—I was waiting to hear the message of the Great Bell that may be sounding its last watches tonight . . . I went on waiting. He went on talking.

I was no longer interested in what he was saying. The seed of doubt had borne its fruit. He could talk of this or he could talk of that. He could say one thing or the other. I was waiting for facts . . . for the fact, the crudely palpable event that I could touch with my fingers . . . the wound in his side, in his heart, in which I could place my hand . . . More than for the great Iron Bell I was listening for the ringing of the night bell at my gate . . . for the arrival of the yellow handkerchief of flimsy silk . . . *before* the double stroke of the second watch.

The second watch sounded, far away over the City. He appeared to have heard nothing, though he was sitting right beside me. I wondered—must I alert him?

No message appeared. No ringing at my gate. Not one

footfall in the street outside, though the frozen ground would have given ample warning ... He seemed to listen for something for a moment, then he went on talking. He was talking, just like his best days ... But for the first time I had no desire to note down or even to remember what he was telling me.

Chinese hours being twice as long as our own, it was in a somewhat nervous state that I waited for the three strokes of the third watch. She would still come, of course, although her handkerchief had not preceded Her, for he was here and showed no sign of going to Her on this—as I had decided—tragic night. Until then, I thought, let him go on talking. I was all ears—but for the silence beyond his words, for the voiceless clarity of the winter night, for the sound of the bell that would tell me in its mechanical, peremptory way whether She, tonight, would be faithful or not, whether he whom I had called my friend was worthy of friendship ... or not ...

I waited ... until ...

"The bell. The third watch."

I let the sound die away. I listened for a while longer. I gave him the benefit of a moment of silence. Nothing. My gate remained closed. He had lied to me. What he had told me and promised me would happen had failed to happen. Was everything he had told me true or was it false? My turn, I thought, to take up the story, the stories ... and not in confidence, either.

But then I remembered—he is in my house. He is my guest. Even the anthropophagi respect their guests, or cook them before they eat them ... I changed my tack and challenged him in my normal tone of voice, which I am told is full of insolent politeness.

"I say, René Leys, you don't appear to realize the time."

No answer.

"We were," I pursued, "to have been visited at ten o'clock by a yellow handkerchief, and at twelve midnight by Her, the Other Woman, your Number One ... It is precisely five past twelve."

He said nothing.

"You asked me once before," I continued, "whether you might count on me, I believe?"

That made him sit up.

"Oh yes!" he said immediately. "I so much wanted to be able to count on you!"

"Splendid. As a friend?"

"Oh yes—as a friend."

"Good. Well, allow me in turn to . . . confide in you . . . as a friend . . . Allow me to tell you this—I no longer understand the first thing about all the stories you tell me, I no longer believe a word of them, and rather than complain of the fact to Jarignoux as he complained to me about having lent you . . . a small sum of money I prefer to speak frankly and to your face . . . on this night which from now on is ours to do as we like with . . ."

"All right. Let's talk . . ."

"It's getting a bit hot and stuffy in here. Shall we go outside? We'll be more at our ease."

He was on his feet before I was, and on his way out. I stopped him.

"What if by some extraordinary chance *She* should come and find no one here?" I asked.

"Whom are you talking about?"

"Why—Her . . ."

He heaved an enormous, involuntary sigh and said, "That's all over now."

We went out into the street beneath the moon's cooling shower, that dazzling rain that pours down from Pei-king's pellucid winter sky. It was astonishingly, piercingly clear. Purple shadows. You could "read a book," as the saying goes . . . Would our exchange, I hoped, be perhaps less "novelistic," less day-to-day? That light scoured every corner and gave even the rubbish heaps a bluish tinge . . . Should we, I wondered, glimpse jewels that the mighty sun and its shadows had never yet divulged?

It was bitterly cold, and René Leys, in his hurry to be outside, had forgotten that one does not go out without one's fur any more. He was shivering in a thin overcoat. And the light took on a special pallor on his face. All I could see of it was his distended eyes that the light failed to invade . . . A chance observation . . . And his look of real suffering. Feelings! Reflections! Stop playing about, I told myself, or play harder.

"Before I go a step further," I said, and I did not care if I was being too harsh, "I need to know three things. If I am utterly wrong, stop me. If my questions offend you, you have the right not to answer them. If I am right, you answer. Agreed?"

He indicated that he agreed.

"First question. How did you become the friend and companion of . . . not Her . . . not the Regent . . . but Himself? I mean —how did you get into the Palace to begin with?"

No answer.

"Second question. What was the exact sum that you paid out to gain access . . . to the very heart of the center of the Within—to Her? Where is the receipt that admitted you?"

"I . . ." He made an effort. "I've . . . lost it."

This I knew. I have it myself and do not intend to part with it.

"Third question. Have you—yes or no—lain with the Empress?"

I deliberately used this passive yet so active verb because I wanted whatever happened to goad him into replying—even if it had to be a categorical denial . . .

He looked at me, and answered simply and levelly, "Yes. I've lain with Her."

And I asked simply and levelly, "The proof?"

And he, with complete naturalness, answered, "The proof? Why—the child."

"Ah!"

"It's a boy, too. The chief eunuch, Ma, rang me at the Central Bureau of the S.P. a week ago to tell me—almost the moment he'd been born. I haven't seen him. He looks like me . . . He has a European nose."

That aggravating habit of having an answer to everything!

I began to feel he was in the wrong place and asked him, "Why are you here?"

He did not understand. He looked puzzled. I explained: a husband and father who left his family to fend for themselves on such a night . . . ?

"Yes, you're right," he agreed. "I ought to be there . . ." And he gave me a look of such gravity, of such supreme penitence beneath that pitiless sky that I faltered, afraid at the depths behind those eyes . . . I made my voice less severe.

"Come—don't worry," I said consolingly. "None of those things we've feared will happen tonight . . . It's always like that in China . . . The abdication will be negotiated in the most amicable manner . . . Indeed it may already have taken place . . . It's late. Too late for there to be time to burn the Palace tonight . . . No, there'll be no massacre tonight . . . Still, let me give you a piece of advice, which is to be less frightened of wells and of chemical bombs that harm no one but their emissaries and rather more on the lookout, in the interests of your own personal safety, for a certain culinary danger of which you appear to be utterly unaware . . . and have never mentioned to me, but which here in China is a . . . traditional method of . . ."

He was listening with such seriousness that I suddenly had the feeling I should stop . . . But it was really too absurdly out of place, I thought.

And I went on, "Did you never, in your 'stories,' think of poison?"

A moment passed before he replied quite calmly, "No. You're right. I shall bear it in mind. Thank you for mentioning it to me."

He came back with me, walking with the easy gait of one who has been out for a stroll and is now returning home. He has come back with me, quietly and a little shamefacedly, to seek shelter on this night that he has himself given me to understand is decisive . . . I left him with a fresh access of ill-humor, humiliated to have such a guest under my roof at such a moment.

A winter morning just like any other. Nothing happened in the night. Nothing at all. For the first time Pei-king has disappointed me: the City did not burn last night.

Such contemptibility defies belief . . . Is it such a little thing, then, to surrender the powers of Heaven and transfer them to the powers of this world? The five-year-old Emperor, with the Regent's soft, fat fingers guiding his hand, "let drop from his brush" the gesture that confers on the Dictator, Yuan Shih-kai, full powers for the Happiness of the People and the care and nurture of the Empire . . . After which they no doubt all returned to their respective apartments and slept soundly.

It may be indiscreet or clumsy of me to wake at this hour . . . for all that it is an historic one. And to be suddenly as lucid as the "great dry winter sky." It is a deep, deep sleep I am waking from. For the first time the day is not what I expected. Pei-king is no longer the haunt of my dreams. My bad mood invading and besieging the very Palace itself, I even begin to doubt that I ever wanted to set foot inside it!

As if I had spent the night drinking too much of that terrible Belgian champagne, my mouth feels awful and my thoughts feel worse. I wish I could say I had a really raging headache to excuse the truly nauseating state of my thoughts . . . I write this with a peevish pen, and without risking a political inquiry today I propose to go back to bed again as the dawn rises over one of my last days in Pei-king. Tonight or tomorrow I shall pack my bags.

I have just reread the first sheet of this manuscript and found myself underlining—the gesture was involuntary—the words: "*I shall know no more . . . I shall retire from the field . . .*"

And adding in a quite different hand: ". . . and I do not wish to know any more."

As part of regularizing my accounts I rode up to the north of the Tatar City to pay Master Wang his final month's fees, which he received with astonished gratitude. Having asked for refuge under my roof he considered himself—or so I understood—as it were, morally my tenant . . . and as such it was he . . . who ought to be . . .

I stemmed this flood of politeness by confessing that I should shortly be leaving my house in the "southeastern corner," and probably the Capital as well, and returning to my "kingdom" . . . but that I did not want to leave him without a European refuge should he ever again be in need of one. I gave him a card to add to his collection, and assured him that it would open the doors of France to him at the well-known address of her Legation.

To my great surprise he accepted both the card and the refuge. Everything is quiet now and "business" will soon be as usual. The Regent's decree of abdication was in yesterday evening's papers.

The account settled, it remained only for me to bid my old tutor farewell and, profiting as much as possible from his lessons, to attempt to translate, without unwarranted irony, the Imperial decree of which the text is anyone's for "a copper"—

the price of a slice of watermelon (already sucked) down in the market!

Positively my last duty in this quarter I am leaving for-ever—for my decision is taken and the furniture remover noti-fied—was to say my good-byes to my neighbor Jarignoux. Fail-ing the Princes of the Blood I thought perhaps one who has sold his European blood could give me the commercial reason be-hind this (doubtless paid) epilogue of the abdication, this waiver, this withdrawal without a fuss . . .

Just as I rang at his gate he came out of it.

"Hey!" he exclaimed. "I was just coming round to see you! You . . . haven't heard what's happened, I suppose?"

"No. Nothing's happened at all!"

"Ah, poor Mr. Leys . . ."

All right, I told him—I could guess: Grocer Leys, twice married, found himself a second time deceived.

"But I don't mean the father. I'm talking about poor Mr. René . . ."

"What about him?"

"Poor boy . . . He was in and out of your house all the time, wasn't he? He was found dead this morning."

Was that all, I thought—just another story to add to the many he has already told me so well . . . ?

Jarignoux was clearly waiting for some reaction. It was too good a moment to resist . . .

"Tell me, Mr. Jarignoux, am I right in assuming it was René Leys himself that instructed you to inform me of his demise?"

"Eh?" was all he could say. He had lost his all-round idiot's look and was exasperating me by trying on the mask of the "decent sort."

"I said: was it René Leys that gave you this information?" I wondered incidentally where he was, thinking he had been faithful to my hospitality for the last two nights.

Befuddled by my response, Jarignoux could only stutter,

"But I tell you I've just seen him on his bed . . . You know him so well—go and see for yourself!"

And the worthy fellow, deeply moved, went on to explain that René Leys' boy had called on him at about eight a.m. and said he thought that "his master's illness" was lasting longer than usual this morning . . .

His "illness!" I realized immediately that René Leys had fainted again. Lack of the expected emotions, no doubt.

Or had I perhaps been a bit rough with him the other day, I wondered, with my three-point interrogatory? And now he had passed out . ∴. for a little too long . . . overdoing it . . . I decided to go and bring him round. I owe him that, I thought.

I went. I have just come back. René Leys did not wake up. For the first time Jarignoux is right: René Leys is dead. I shall never forget this morning. This ghastly Pei-king, already practically a republic, that revolutionary sky . . . His boy, who was paler even than he—afraid that some charge would be brought against him?—was crying like a sentimental dog. The house was open and unguarded. The boy must have known what was what because he did not beseech me in my European wisdom to make his master well again, and he appeared to have spared him the usual last-minute remedies practiced in China (needles stuck in all over the place) . . .

René Leys' face was just as I remembered it from his former fainting fits . . . of which this was the fourth. A handsome, set, relaxed expression no longer tensed in striving after the goal, whatever it might be. The eyes were wide open, and more than ever—and now forever—there was that swallowing-up of the entire iris by the darkness of the pupil . . . I did not close them, letting them play out their bewitching role to the end in the incorruptible charm of that face. I undressed him to find out the cause of death before the doctors should start interfering. René Leys effectively "died of poison" for I found no trace of a wound anywhere . . . The architecture of his body surprised me—so much strength couched in such suppleness!

The perfection of symmetrical elegance . . . Tracing the line of his hips and thighs I could see the secret of his grip on that wild horse of his, and even in their relaxed state his arms told me how he would have tamed and subdued women had he lived! Just brown enough not to be dubbed "white" by the yellow Chinese . . . And a dullness to that already-cold skin that was very like the delicate touch of the Chinese epidermis . . .

René Leys, then, intact, already cold, is dead . . . died shortly after leaving me the day before yesterday. But what was the poison?

If I mention my misgivings the doctors will demand an autopsy. Analysis of the stomach contents . . . desecration of that beautiful body I dressed and covered up before I left . . . I shall keep quiet about them. Yet I should like to know—not as a doctor but as a man—the cause of his death.

One thing and one alone of all of the foregoing is certain: René Leys is dead, and it was definitely not a natural death—a concept moreover, that the good Taoist does not admit. When one has lived with a person, when one has ridden hard beside him as I have, one knows his organs were sound. So is one to conclude that he was poisoned by his colleagues, his competitors . . . his rivals . . . ? But I know perfectly well that the Chinese steer clear of fast-acting poison, which is as dangerous for the cook as for his victim, and always avail themselves of the slow poisons they can administer with impunity.

Was he then poisoned . . . by Her?

But why? Granted her "dynastic affairs" have for some time not been going too well. The abdication . . . But she must have been paid off . . . And he "lost everything he had," of course, when his bank crashed. But at seventeen! In the nine months I have known him he has not even changed the tally of his years! That so much can have happened in so short a time!

And the way he said: "Ah well, here we go again!" After all, he was strong enough to do it; even with the fortunes of the Manchus in ruins he was young enough to carve out a completely new future for himself in "European circles" . . . His prodigious talent for assimilation . . . his linguistic gifts—speaking English, Pekingese, Shanghaian, Cantonese, and Pidgin quite at will . . . A few more months and I could have got him into a bank, even a respectable one . . . For a grocer's son—don't let's forget that—he could have made quite a career for himself. Why was he not honest with me? I could certainly have put him on his feet again!

Did he poison himself, then—out of lover's spite? But he was never very deeply in love. What was he doing away from Her on what was supposed to be the Big Tragic Night!

Yet it was the day following that night that he died. The day following that moment in which for the first time I doubted him, in which I challenged him to his face . . . in which I came close to disbelieving him . . . in which he saw his "stories," his whole marvelous history called into question . . . his word contested!

In that case he would have used "leaves of gold," the emperors' death . . . and in point of color a perfect match for his stories . . . The leaf of gold, image and symbol, which alone could not kill in spite of all they say about it but which contains opium . . . He despised opium.

This doubt . . . If he had left a will, something in writing . . . But there was nothing, not even any furniture, only that narrow little bed in his father's old house. And he distrusted that house to which so many merchants had access . . .

There is nothing here either, except two letters already transcribed . . .

And this enigmatic receipt for his "first night of love in the Palace"—which he thought was lost . . . nor did I undeceive him. I have already attempted to decipher it. Am I a bad pupil, or is the homework too hard? The characters represent a series of the most alarming objects: knives, a barbed spear, eyes placed lengthwise or vertically, flowers, rat's teeth, women hiding their bellies, wells, pits, tombs, the stopped-up holes of some lid . . . a magic crucible . . . an empty mouth . . . a boat . . . Where in all this is the legend "First night of love in the Palace"?

Should I have it translated? But if it is a forgery—or possibly just an old household bill—what an ass I shall look! If it really is . . . that . . . then what a betrayal of him who can no longer prevent it . . . and no longer give account of himself!

Or is it simply that another hand than his wrote it? For calligraphy was high on the list of his astounding gifts . . .

And so I find myself brought face to face with my only valid witness—this manuscript, of which nine months ago I hoped to "make a book," and which I now regard with a suspicion that is the deeper for all it contains. I recollect that he was not unaware of its existence. In fact he once asked me to be sure I kept it up. With his approval, then, and dedicating it to his memory, I turn back and for the first time read it through from beginning to end . . .

And, for the last time, close it—having penned what follows.

I have read this manuscript through word by word with an ever-deepening emotion and sense of involvement, discarding alike my doubts and suspicions—and establishing with certainty the fact of my own guilt.

René Leys did not kill himself. *They* did not poison him. And yet he clearly died of poison. This paradox is in fact the truest of confessions. The poison: it was *I* that offered it to him —and with the worst will in the world! It was from me that he received it, accepted it, drank it . . . and that from the very moment of our first meeting . . .

René Leys, the thrifty son of a Belgian grocer, hardly had a thought for the Chinese, and even less for the Palace, when for the first time I made him my confidant regarding the mysteries of the Forbidden City . . . though it is true that his response exceeded my expectations right from the start. It was I who, on the strength of Master Wang, first spoke to him of the existence of a Secret Police. A few days later he was a member of it, and a few months later he had enlisted me. For the attempts on the Regent's life I decline responsibility—they were in all the papers for anyone to read—but I do charge myself with repeatedly asking this question: "Tell me, Leys—is it possible for a Manchu woman to be loved by a European, and . . . ?" And three weeks later he was loved by a Manchu woman . . .

Lastly and most grievously I accuse myself of having fed him exactly four days ago that too-suggestive cue: "Don't forget poison . . ." He replied, "Thank you for mentioning it to me," made the suggestion his, and abode by it.

He always abode by what he said. That searing interrogatory in the clear, cold night could never have led anywhere. I asked him, "Yes or no—have you . . . ?" But I should have been mortally disappointed had he disowned his (even invented) deeds; I trembled more than he did at feeling the whole splendid edifice teeter . . . I could hear his reply before he gave it; in ruthlessly disabusing me he would have the more bitterly deceived me. He abode by his word and it may be by my suggestions . . .

Everything I said, he did, Chinese fashion, for with his death he has just given me, Chinese fashion, the best proof—that he preferred to lose his life if it meant saving face . . . if it was the only way of not being false either to himself or to me, of neither breaking faith nor forfeiting my esteem . . . Is it all true, then—"Chinese fashion"?

And the proof I asked for . . . set up . . . the crucial proof —the child . . . which he himself said was "a fine boy" . . . Even if the child is alive and viable . . . why should I suddenly find myself counting on my fingers . . . up to nine? The interval between my suggestion and the child's birth does seem a bit short . . . This boy is definitely a surprise . . . But share and share alike! My share . . . Ah—shall I ever know how much of him came from me?

There remain those inexplicable moments . . . glimpses, flashes . . . insights, words no one could have made up, things no one could have fabricated . . . All his confidences really did inhabit an essential Palace built upon the most magnificent foundations . . . And the sets he conjured up . . . and that teeming ceremonial and secret Pekingese life that no truth as officially known will ever begin to suspect . . .

Now I come to think about it, his share is really very much richer than my own ... The youth to have dared so much! The faith, possibly, to have accomplished it ... And here am I, alive, toting my doubts around his death bed like a smoky lamp ... when, if I should keep faith with him—it has suddenly dawned on me—I ought to start by remembering his words: that other, the Emperor, died without a friend beside him ... "I was his friend," René Leys told me with shattering emphasis ...

I was his friend—I ought to say with the same emphasis, the same loyal regret, without going any further into what exactly our friendship consisted in ... for fear of killing him, or of killing him a second time ... or—which would be even more unpardonable—of being suddenly called upon to answer my doubt myself and finally pronounce: yes or no?

Pei-king, 1 November 1913 to 31 January 1914.

Notes

[1] The historian Hugh Trevor Roper has drawn attention to an "uncanny parallel" between Maurice Roy and the British sinologist Sir Edmund Backhouse (1873-1944), who towards the end of his life wrote a lurid account of his own extremely intimate relations with the Chinese imperial court. To reveal more details here would be to risk spoiling Segalen's game. The reader is warmly recommended to consult Hugh Trevor Roper's *Hermit of Peking: The Hidden Life of Sir Edmund Backhouse* (London: Macmillan, 1976; New York: Knopf, 1977), where the reference to *René Leys* occurs in Chaper 15 [Tr.].

[1a] The quotations and much of the information contained in this introduction are taken from Henry Bouillier, *Victor Segalen*, Paris, 1961.

[2] The author, remember, is French (Tr.).

[3] Paul Féval (1817–87), a prolific author of adventure stories and melodramas (Tr.).

[4] 1851–62. The French Second Empire dated from 1852 to 1870 (Tr.).

[5] The Bell Tower is thought to stand at what used to be the center of Kublai Khan's city of Khanbaliq (Tr.).

[6] A reference to the legendary site of the martyrdom of St. Denis and his companions—better known as Montmartre (Tr.).

[7] Sadi Carnot was President of France from 1887 to 1894, *i.e.* through the period of the Boulangist disturbances. He survived, only to be assassinated by an anarchist on 24 June 1894 (Tr.).

[8] The verb implied is presumably *dépuceler,* Joan of Arc being known in French as "La Pucelle d'Orléans" (Tr.).

[9] The *zaïmph,* on which the safety of Carthage was held to depend, was the sacred veil of the goddess Tanit. It was stolen by Matho, one of the leaders of the Carthaginian mercenaries in their revolt against Carthage following the 1st Punic War in 241 B.C.—and the principal figure in Flaubert's *Salammbô* (Tr.).

[10] The exchange referred to took place after the fall of the Bastille on 14 July 1789 and went as follows:

LOUIS XVI: *C'est une révolte?*

DUC DE LA ROCHEFOUCAULD-LIANCOURT: *Non, Sire, c'est une révolution.* (Tr.).